A Father's Love

A story of reflection

by Lavita Stokes

 www.trafford.com

North America & international
toll-free: 1 888 232 4444 (USA & Canada)
phone: 250 383 6864 ♦ fax: 812 355 4082

Dedication

This book is dedicated to my husband Ronnie who has been my driving force and my rock. To my four beautiful children, my precious gifts from God. They have taught me patience, acceptance and given me unconditional love. Having them has made me see what it feels like to truly love and be loved and to see how precious life is. To my late grandmother (momma), & my late sister. Momma taught me to accept me for who I am and the shining light I can be to others. She instilled in me strength and courage, because of her I am who I am today. A loving wife, mother and friend.

My two soldiers, my protectors both now deceased, but I know they are still guiding me. My late great-grandfather George Fanning, and my late great-uncle Ernest Baynes. From the time we first met loved me like I was his own daughter. He became the father I never had.

To all the fatherless daughters and sons of the world. I hope this book will touch your hearts and you draw strength from my story knowing that you are not alone and despite life's obstacles you can rise above the storm. Never let life's adversities control who you are and detour you from reaching your destiny in life.

Take the adversity and turn it into a positive and by doing so you will not only free yourself, but inspire others as well.

Acknowledgements

Thank you to all my beautiful Girlfriends who are always there when I need a shoulder to lean on or an ear just to listen. Your love and belief in me helped me to believe in myself. Tracee Garrett and Anna Quevedo for getting me started. To all who have touched my life in a special way, through a prayer said, a word of encouragement given, a hug when I needed one the most, a shoulder to cry on or an ear to listen when I needed a friend. I say Thank you for all your Love and Support. A special thank you to my sister ShaRhonda Brown who believed in me when I wanted to give up. Despite all the obstacles I had to endure to bring my dream of writing this book into reality. Her encouragement and dedication along with her relentless support helped me turn my dream into an actual reality. Without her this would not have been possible.

Intro

This is a heartwarming story about courage and the ability to overcome pain from the past. Meet Lavita, a woman who reflects on the absence of her Biological Father. Rejected and often filled with bitterness she learns to draw strength from God and Family. Ultimately, she realizes that only through forgiveness can she gain healing and liberty from her past. Though often difficult, this journey is necessary, if she is to give love and affection so desperately sought from her own children.

Preface

In modern society there is often an acute awareness of the statistics revealed publicly, as it relates to absentee Fathers. While those statistics serve the purpose of educating one on the demographic data associated with absentee fathers, they don't fully reveal the entire picture. Part of what is not measured is the distinct dynamics of social conditions. In every single parent home there are specific circumstances that have influenced the condition that leads to abandoned children. There are single parent homes that may have shared overlapping patterns, but make no mistake, each situation is unique. Beyond the statistics, there exists authentic, children, bearers of innocent eye's and tender hearts. In the book, "A Father's love" we find one such innocent soul simply longing to be loved. Many years after the eyes are no longer innocent there remains a longing to be wrapped up in a Father's affectionate arms. Time does not diminish the need to be supported emotionally, spiritually, and provided with a reference point of identity for that child.

Meet a young woman who takes a period of time to reflect upon her own painfully raw childhood experience. While the reader may not have the ability to see visible pictures, the objective is to create word imagery by traveling through the halls of "past pain and baggage," to better understand the human aspect that lies behind the statistic.

Lavita is a mother who adores her children and pours her love and energy into creating a nurturing environment for each one of them. In fact, it is through her children that she learns that she has yet to move beyond her yearning for a Father who never fully acknowledged her. Despite the fact that God placed individuals in her life to act in a surrogate role, including a compassionate husband, she yet hurts. This is her story, it may also be your story, and from a broader perspective it is a tragic human story. But tragedy is only the first half because on the other side of pain exists the possibility of redemption. Beyond the statistics, beyond the cold facts, there is a lesson learned about the importance of Fatherhood, of taking responsibility. There is much to be learned about the dynamic and life changing power of, "A Father's Love."

Chapter 1: The Beginning

I am the Innocent

You were not spoken of or even mentioned
You did not appear
Therefore you did not exist
I am the innocent
Years later I wanted to know your part of me
I wanted to know Part of your history, which is part of mine
I wanted to know our part that made me who I am
I found you so I called
You had developed selective amnesia
You said, "I don't know anything about the situation."
I am the innocent
I told one of my sisters's what you said
She said not to be troubled
You are like some of the other males in this world
You are a drive by shooter
I am the innocent
I found someone else from your past
That said you are part of me and I am part of you
I have kinships
She'll contact them to see if we could meet
She had papers from the court system
That said we are connected
She knew that...
I am innocent
I am your sperm donation
I am your contribution to this world's population
I am your deception, your infidelity
I am your forgotten
I am the part of you that you left behind
I am the victim of your crime
I am...
I am...
THE INNOCENT

R. Marshell Hall

As I look out my bedroom window, the sky appears dark before me. My heart reflects a picture similar to the sky it is also dark and heavy. I am gravely aware that deep within me throbs' a pain that is both raw and intense. It appears as though it might rain. Gazing absently at the calendar I notice it is the first day of spring, yet it remains dreary outside. The trees are blowing like dandelions in response to the slight yet persistent flurry of wind. It is the first day of spring when budding flowers should be pushing their imaginative heads, through the ground. Instead it looks like it is going to be one of those days were you just want to curl up in your bed with a good book. The first day of spring, colorful leaves should be on the trees and my grass should be noticeably beginning to take on the lush colors of green. Instead, all that greets my shadowy presence is a gray and gloomy sky. Perhaps it may rain at any moment. Reflecting yet again on my own internal pain and dark sky, the tears begin to tumble down without shame.

My mind begins to rotate rapidly backwards through an emotional and historic past, for the purpose of reflecting on how I arrived at this place. I note the fact that my son Ronnie Jr. is such a sensitive soul. He always manages to say or do something that can elicit an unexpected response within me. I seldom welcome the recurrence of veiled emotions I thought were long ago submerged like sand into the ocean. These sand particles of emotion symbolize feelings of abandonment. The sea bed is filled with shells of regret and pain from not having the love or acknowledgment of a father. Ronnie Jr. and I share a familiar bond that unfortunately I was not able to experience with my biological father. Although scarcely personally acknowledged, this has been the source of a deep wound that goes soul deep. I thought these feelings were gone but realized I was mistaken.

In order to better help you understand my story, let me tell you a little more about my son. The birth of my son was indeed one of God's greatest miracles in my life. From as far back as I can remember I longed to give birth to a son. Perhaps deep down in my heart I felt that the love of a son would cure the ailment caused by the absence of fatherly affection. Although the desire for such a bond is difficult to explain the importance it held in my life cannot be overstated. From the moment Ronnie Jr. was born there was a special mother-son bond that we shared. I felt that it was validation of God's love. Further, I believe it was a result of countless prayer petitions sent up to God for a son.

I am always careful to acknowledge and tell people that prior to the birth of Ronnie I was blessed with two beautiful girls, Laurel and Amber and after Ronnie a third little angel named Sydney. From my three daughters I learned the importance of selfless love for a human being other than my husband. They also taught me patience and the importance of bonding through role play. Through activities with them, tea parties with the best imaginary tea and hours of playful dialogue, they sparked the reemergence of my own imagination. In essence, my girls both prepared and equipped me for the birth of Ronnie Jr. Of all the things that they taught me the importance of "Unconditional Love," probably stands out the most. According to Wikipedia, Harold W. Becker, author and founder of The Love Foundation, Inc., defines Unconditional Love as *"an unlimited way of being."* From his book of the same title, Becker goes on to say that *"the greatest power known to man is that of unconditional love."* (Unknown) This surreal yet present universe was only fully realized through interaction and bonding with my children. They love me regardless of whatever faults I may have and my son was no exception. I was so appreciative of that unconditional love that I saw him as my God sent angel. From the time he was born his smile and sensitivity would attract even the most calloused individuals. Although he did have some health related complications, he was able to overcome them by the Grace of God. No matter how old he gets, just like his father, he will always be mommy's cuddly little teddy bear. Both Ronnie Jr. and his Father crave affection, hugs, and plenty of kisses. In essence, they equate human touch with love. I told Ronnie Jr. his wife is going to have her hands full!

All my children are beautiful both inside and out, their spirits radiate and produce positive energy. They also appreciate being around family and eagerly anticipate the various family get togethers. It's funny because particularly the girls have never really asked about the existence of their grandfather. That would include either my biological father or the father of my husband. In contrast, it has been my son who has most felt the void as a result of not having any biological grandfather in his life.

From the time Ronnie Jr. was two years old he would often ask, *"Mommy why don't I have a grandpa?"* On one occasion, the two of us were enjoying a movie aptly titled, "The Color of Love." One of the principle characters in the movie was a noticeably charismatic yet gentle grandfather figure. Upon seeing this character, Ronnie immediately began to wonder aloud why he didn't have a grandpa like the other kids he saw.

My two older daughters knew their biological grandfather on my husband's side but can't recall specific details pertaining to his life. This is due to the fact that he passed away when they were barely two and four years old respectively. When asked if they remember their Grandpa Stokes their response is text-book, *"Mom we were way too young to remember Grandpa."* Much of their unfamiliarity with my father is due to a much thornier scenario. It is primarily influenced by the fact that I never had a relationship with my Father, so he was absent from my children's lives. Deep inside I know my son and my Father in law would have gotten along great, had he not passed before Ronnie Jr's birth.

It was always uncomfortable and tricky trying to explain to my son that his grandfather was in heaven. This was simply an explanation that he was not prepared or willing to hear. Sometimes he would respond, *"I'm going to go to heaven so that I can see my grandpa. I want him to take me fishing."* Then I would have to respond by saying,

"Ronnie that is impossible, if you went to heaven then who would take care of mommy?" I would also remind him that I would be lost without him.

My daughters never really asked about the whereabouts of my biological father until after we received the news from my sister that he had passed away. It was after that unfortunate event that my son really felt the void and sense of longing for a grandfather. He did not really care what grandpa looked like; he just wanted to experience the same modeled grandpa-grandson relationships that he saw everyday both on the screen and in real life.

Reflecting again on that night we watched the movie, "<u>The Color of Love</u>," several significant moments stick out. I remember him asking, *"Mommy can I lay in your bed before you tuck me in?"* I had just finished tucking my youngest daughter safely into her bed not long ago. Moments later I was unwinding in my room watching the movie when in walked Ronnie Jr. As I saw his tiny figure standing apprehensively in the doorway, I imagined my "little man" climbing out of his bed. Unsure of mommy's reaction, he probably took small, slightly unsure, measured steps down the hall until he arrived at the door. Once he arrived at the door and studied my face for a few minutes he gained the necessary confidence to enter, just as he has done so many times before. Then just as I have so often responded in the past, I said, *"Ronnie you can stay in mommy and daddy's room for a little while then mommy will tuck you in to your bed, ok?"*

This calculated compromise I agreed to with the awareness that he usually would fall asleep during the movie. Subsequently, as the end credits rolled he was counting sheep. I would then simply lift his limp body and carefully take measured steps down the same hall so as not to wake him. Upon reaching his bedroom I would bend down carefully placing him into his bed.

However, on that particular night that we watched, "The Color of Love" Ronnie Jr. seemed more attentive than any other nights. My hopes of him falling fast asleep during the movie began to gradually dissolve. What kept him engaged in the movie I believe was the grandfather character. He further reinforced this notion by asking, *"Mommy where is grandpa, I want to see him?"* I could sense that my traditional and measured *"Heaven"* response just would not suffice. Not this time. His entire being, remained transfixed on the character grandpa throughout the movie. Towards the end I began to experience feelings of guilt. The questions and longing so powerfully articulated by such a young boy also represented my own stubborn and quietly brewing pain resulting from my father's absence. Secretly, and somewhat embarrassed, I chided myself for not tucking him in before the movie had begun. Perhaps with him tucked away in his bed, I too could leave my unwanted emotions secretly and safely tucked away in the hardening crevice of my heart. At the conclusion of the movie the dam broke. Crocodile tears that had slowly begun to swell in his eyes now were gushing uninhibited down his "china like" ebony face. As you can probably imagine I was too caught off guard to react.

The only response I could offer came in the form of love that only Ronnie Jr. could truly appreciate. That response was that familiar and comforting connection of human touch. I grabbed him and held him so tightly for a moment I could feel the shape of his skeletal system. The contour, hardness and very formation of his bones seemed in danger of being crushed in a moments' notice. His little heart was thumping and bumping so loudly it could have been the drums of a marching band funeral procession.

Then I began to rock him. Our joined figures were together swaying like the trees outside underneath an overcast sky. Scarcely hours before any storm, it's often dark outside. In similar fashion there was an emotional storm that filled both Ronnie Jr. and my life with sadness and yes, even anger. As I rocked him I softly whispered a loving yet nervous inquiry into his ear, *"Ronnie can you tell mommy what's wrong?"* Somehow perhaps I wanted him to say anything but the truth that we both already knew was the source of both of our pain. As I searched for a way to comfort this innocent child, my son, the only thought that came to mind was to call my mother in law.

Let me give you a little history as to the reason why my mother-in-law was my go to person during this difficult evening. Ronnie shared such a close bond with his grandmother ever since he was born that I knew if anyone could calm his troubled spirit besides me she could. She would continuously spoil him with kisses, hugs, and while in her presence he grew accustomed to being showered with affection. It gave her great pride to see him eat, because boy he certainly loves food and has a hearty appetite. My mother-in-law has always said that my son is the spitting image of his father, when he was a little boy. Whenever grandma was scheduled to visit you could see the anticipation building in little Ronnie Jr.'s eyes. From the moment he could write and spell he has written her letters just to see how she was doing. His letters were often funny shaped with squiggly lines, but you would think he was writing a college dissertation the way his forehead wrinkled as wrote.

Additionally, he would often send her drawings that he made carefully attaching little notes to let her know that he was thinking about her. Did I mention that his future wife would have her hands full? Also, he waits with expectancy for our family to go visit her at her house. Once he arrives to her home rather than bound about from the inside to the outside and back again, he often just stay's up under his Grandmother. The irony is that both my husband and he are the exact same way, so the apple didn't fall far from the tree. I privately hoped that Ronnie Jr's relationship with his Grandmother would somehow ease the pain and void left by the absence of my own father.

Now that you have some basic history regarding their relationship; you should have a better understanding as to the impact she has on him. Once reached, her words seemed to just soothe and comfort him, his demeanor seemed to brighten. She was often just as surprised as I was to discover the level of sensitivity displayed by a child so young, regarding not having his grandfather. After what seemed like an eternity, and only when she felt he was calm, she wished us both *"good night."* As I carefully hung the phone up I turned to Ronnie and again tenderly kissed him on the forehead. Even though he had calmed significantly I could still here him softly crying and his little body seemed to react to every tearful whimper. Inside I could again feel my own emotions starting to swell as I deeply ached inside.

It hurt not knowing the love of my father and not having his presence in the life of my son, his grandson. It is another dimension of absentee fathers, the impact that is often felt by the next generation. Thinking about the emotions that both my son and I felt was like treading water and feeling your lungs burn. Only, judging by the way I felt we were no longer treading water we were actually drowning with no life preservers. It was simultaneously exhausting and suffocating at the same time. My son eventually cried himself to sleep. As he lay there, sleeping next to me I felt so empty, so lost. Suddenly many thoughts begin to flood my mind. I had always asked myself, ever since I could remember *who needs a father anyway?* Yet deep down inside I knew that in fact, I did. I needed a father, a daddy, comforting arms and answers, especially at this moment with Ronnie Jr.

Ronnie Jr. relished imagining things that he would do if he did have a grandfather. Things like going on fishing trips, taking walks in the park, or doing activities similar to the ones that he did with his father. It is as though by imagining he could actually smell the salt water that contained the fish, or feel the texture of the bark that coated the trees in the park. He wanted to experience such magical moments with a grandfather, his grandfather. When my son would ask about his grandfather I would usually just change the subject as quickly as possible. One of the ways that I tried to compensate was by highlighting Grandpa Stokes, my husbands' father. I would say, *"Grandpa Stokes would have enjoyed hanging out with you honey, you two would have been best buddies."* Then I would follow that statement up by sharing pictures of Grandpa Stokes and entertaining him with video footage we had captured of him. In contrast, I could not show him pictures of my father because I did not have any pictures... and it would have hurt too much. Throughout the book I am going to offer tips which I believe will be helpful for Dads, or even surrogate father figures who play a significant role in the lives of children.

TIP 1: *Hugs, hugs and more hugs:* Physical touch is so important in a child's development; you should continue to hug your children every day from infancy into adulthood. Hugs are the glue that bonds both parent and child together. As was the case with Ronnie Jr., it is the silent technique allowing both parties to simply but effectively say, *"I love you unconditionally no matter what."* And remember even though you may have verbalized this phrase just last week, children need continual reinforcement. Especially if you are a birth dad who is currently either uninvolved or under involved in your child's life. Do what you can to set aside differences with the mother and be there for your children. Also, if you are a surrogate father figure, by default your role is to help rebuild that child's self-esteem and sense of security.

Chapter 2: Momma

Big Momma

When she walked into a room

She was so unassuming

Never demanded attention

Only wanted to bless

Her words were few

And far between

Her love immaculate

Creased at the seams

Big Momma was the kind

That would never cause a scene

I found love in her presence

She awakened my dream

The straightest distance between hopelessness

And the will to survive

Is found in the solace, love

And tireless drive

Of My "Big Momma"

Rudo

*I*t was my maternal grandmother who took on the responsibility of raising me. I called her "Momma" and my son took to calling her "Big Momma." Physically, Momma was about 5' 5" possibly shorter and she was also noticeably plump. While being diminutive from a physical standpoint, she was yet exceedingly tall in stature when it came to her ability to love people. When I was a child there came a time when my biological mother, *Dora's*, addiction to the street life made her incapable of caring for me, my brothers, and my sisters. As fate would have it, Momma took on the role of surrogate mother. Momma though small in stature, embodied the essence of one who is gentle, uncompromisingly caring, and warm in spirit. She would never purposefully seek to harm a soul and typically avoided confrontation of any kind.

Although Dora was in and out of the home somewhat sporadically, she did manage to give Momma money to care for us. As a result, even though times were hard economically, somehow, we never went without food, or shelter. While Dora wasn't there for us physically, there remained an invisible yet noticeable divide between her and me. Usually there was minimal interaction between us while occupying the same space. For my part I intentionally chose to distance myself from her both psychologically and emotionally. Perhaps it was simply a defense mechanism, I really don't know. In terms of the whereabouts of my biological father, he simply was not present. His life was similar to that of tumbleweed it blew where the momentum propelled it. Through it all Momma was there, raising five grand-children. She was one of those amazing individuals that God used to fill the void left by the absence of my father. In addition, her affection eased the impact caused by the emotional divide experienced with Dora.

Momma was the driving force in my life, and I loved her dearly. I can relate my feelings for Momma to a popular dedication song entitled, "A Song for Momma," sung by a group "Boyz II Men". This quartet at one time during their heyday was signed to the record label Motown. This song expresses gratitude for the love and guidance given by a Momma even when times were hard. The appreciation so melodically and poetically articulated in this song although poignant pales in comparison to the way I actually feel about my Momma. Her struggle to raise six grandchildren and simultaneously support her own biological daughter was an amazing feat in and of itself. To watch my Momma persevere every day provided inspiration that continues to sustain me year after year. She would wake up each morning, put her faith in God, and fight with such a fierceness you would think she was in a full scale war. I guess that even though it was not the Revolutionary War, or War on Terrorism, it was a War to save the family, which has just as much if not more merit.

Even though there were times that we did not know where our next meal was coming from, Momma never let on. As a young girl, I observed and mentally noted these selfless acts of sacrifice. Eventually this ignited a fierce flame within me to become a change agent. This stubborn flame that Momma lit burned brightly within me. The desire to put people before self became such a fiery, searing desire it burned even my very heart and spirit. From that moment forward, I determined that if this woman, who could easily be easing off the gas of life sacrificed for me then I would make sure that her efforts were not in vain. No, I was determined that no matter how tedious and gigantic the obstacle, I would not yield. It was my intention to simply become the best granddaughter that I could be.

Momma had a "hard knock life" herself as a child, but you would never know this due to the fact she never spoke about it. One tragedy that she faced was losing her parents when she was very young. The result was that she was raised by relatives, but still her environment was far from supportive and loving. Another obstacle that Momma faced was being placed in foster care at the age of either eleven or twelve years old. Eventually she figured she could do better off by herself and she ran away. She was forced to go outside and face that black sky and the swaying trees for the first time in her life. She did this while not knowing the love of either a mother or a father. Facing the world alone she eventually gained her war stripes because she never gave up hope.

I suppose at the end of the day that is the key in life. That is one of the critical life lessons that I learned from her is to never give up hope. Even when people, be it family, friends, or even acquaintances let you down still maintain determination to complete the task. Learn to live by the phrase *"enterprise-me"*. This in essence is the idea that if no one else does it for you, then learn to do it for yourself. Maybe you are a child that had a difficult upbringing who grew up in either a single parent home or one with a surrogate parent. What matters is not the lack of the love of a mother or father but rather how you react to those circumstances. Momma did it, I am doing it, and we can <u>all</u> do it despite our past circumstances.

I remember Momma once confiding in me about how she wished to expand her horizon, to experience the world at large. This is not only a normal desire but it should be a mandatory component in the educational experience of every young person. This is why I encourage my own children to look beyond their own backyard, because there is a whole new world out there waiting for them. Study abroad programs should be made available to children without regards to their socio-economic background, race, color, or creed. Momma had never truly been anywhere in the world, at least not outside of her tiny little enclave of urban America. She was formally only equipped with a sixth grade education. However when you think of all of her "real life" experiences, she received a PHD in the necessity of **Perseverance Hope and Desire**. Thinking about how much she *desired* to see the world I longed to offer her such an opportunity.

Her words became wet ink that would remain etched deeply within my subconscious, for many years thereafter. Given the fact it takes money to accomplish a goal that substantial, I determined to work hard enough, so that one day I could give her that gift. I visualized placing the actual world like a miniature globe, wrapped in a bow, into her arms. After all, she put her world on pause so that I could experience mine. How great then would it be to actually give her a piece of her world back.

Momma was just *that way*. By *that way* I mean she was selfless to a fault. She was never focused on her needs but simply sought to ensure everyone else's peace and happiness. As long as everyone was getting along then she seemed content. Perhaps she fed off of that positive energy, and from it gained a sense of personal accomplishment. My sister and I used to laugh because one thing about Momma was that she didn't know how to keep a secret to save her life. This was true, especially if it was concerning myself or any of my siblings. She would always leak confidential information to one sibling that the other shared with her privately. The conversation would start something like this, *"Now you know so and so said this and I promised I wouldn't tell,* so don't you go blabbing just wait until they tell you themselves." Now to use a figure of speech, *"ain't that the pot calling the kettle black?"* But that was just Momma's way, a short plump softy she was. Our response was textbook, *"Ok Momma..."* we would begin trying to maintain a truly serious and sacrilegious demeanor, *"we won't tell a soul...honest."* Boy as soon as we got away from Momma we couldn't wait to share that funny tad bit of news to the other sibling. It was like our own little "gossip corner" or something. That is what I mean she wanted an environment of tranquility and love shared by everyone, even to a fault. This became more and more evident to us especially as she matured in age. And because she loved her only child Dora deeply, her support and commitment remained unwavering. Not only would she love her daughter despite the ups and downs, she did this while simultaneously raising her grandchildren.

Momma took pride in raising us and even as we reached adulthood she continued to remain actively involved, helping to raise our children. She was a superstar babysitter particularly for my two oldest daughters when they were just babies. She relished the opportunity to assist me in any way that she could. One thing is for certain too, I knew that when I picked them up no matter what else may have been going on they were coming home clean. Momma bathed and greased those girls with so much baby oil they sparkled like ducks swimming in a grease pond. I always joked with her by telling her, *"Momma when I pick up the girls I have to hold on extra tight because with all the oil that you bathe them in they almost slide right out of my arms!"* She would then laugh so hard her whole body seemed to shake.

As I shared earlier, Momma never truly had the opportunity to see the world, like she may have desired to do. I can recall winning the science fair in the seventh grade; one of the prizes was a trip to a local amusement park. Another perk was that the winner got the opportunity to take a parent along. This would be Momma's first trip, because of course given our shared bond I knew I was going to take her. I will never forget the day of the trip Momma looked very young to me as we boarded the bus for departure. What I remember most is the fact that we both had a blast on the trip!

One highlight that day was when I successfully convinced her to ride the merry-go-round with me. I close my eyes even now and picture her head tilted back as the wind swept across her russet face. She seemed almost "child-like" an innocent in that very enchanted moment. It reminds me of a current commercial advertising a theme amusement park. It shows a mother and a daughter holding hands and enjoying the shared experience of the rides and festivities. When they first enter the theme park, they are seemingly both transformed into little girls, giggling and laughing together. Subsequently, once they exit the theme park, they are once again mother and daughter, but the *child-like* bond and shared memories yet remain. At the tail end of the commercial they both turn to each other and playfully giggle, as though reliving their brief but exhilarating quest. That depiction accurately describes how I felt during that moment with my Momma.

If only for that one instant, I could have one wish, it would have been to change into a professional photographer. This would allow me to capture that nostalgic profile shared by me and Momma and preserve it forever. Then whenever I got sad or despondent I could refer back to that memory and recall brighter days. Regardless, I knew that moment would remain with me forever and therefore my spirit refused to be dampened. On the ride back home, Momma admitted that it was the best time she had ever had. Feeling overjoyed and slightly giddy, I tilted my head back, let the cool wind blow against my hair and blurted out, *"Me too Momma, me too!"* Momma even coined a playfully sweet nickname for me as a child. She called me Reese Cup, because everyone else simply referred to me as Reese for short. I can still hear her melodious voice singing and calling me "Reese Cup".

Momma also rejoiced with the birth, the new life, of every child born into the family. Prior to her passing from this side of life and subsequent presence with her heavenly Father, she was blessed to witness the birth of her 22nd grandchild. During that same time period there was also two great-great granddaughters added to the family. Throughout her life Momma never raised her voice and sometimes, notwithstanding her many wonderful attributes, I wished she had on occasion. I feel like this was her one downfall. It is sort of ironic that a woman who fought so many obstacles to survive in life decided that when it came to her family she would not raise her voice or be "tough." Maybe it was her way of overcompensating for the difficult life that many of us experienced growing up. As matter of fact when she did try to get "tough" and raise her voice we would ask her jokingly, *"Momma were you just trying to get bad with me?"*

The only memory I can ever recall of her scolding me is when I was about twelve and my sister Nina and I were arguing and fighting before bedtime. I think Momma may have been at her wits end that day. Nina kept taunting me, so in protest, I started stomping and throwing things. I just started screaming at the top of my lungs, as

Momma would say. It is always interesting to look at things in retrospect. How silly was it for me to holler out of control simply because my sister would not leave me alone. Needless to say there I was doing it anyway, and not in a soft tone but more of a loud, shrill pitch. To make it even more dramatic I started throwing things and stomping on the bedroom floor, all the while screaming, *"Leave me alone!"* Again in hindsight I should have realized that my protest was not going to end well. I can recall as clear as day Momma storming up those stairs moving quicker than I ever realized was possible. We could have both been stars that day. I should have been nominated for a nighttime Emmy award in a sibling drama series, and Momma for an Olympic Gold medal in the steeple chase. But instead of her reaching for her gold medal Momma reached for me and out of nowhere came a "POW" as her hand made contact with my face.

This was the first time I can ever remember as a child being chastised by my Momma. Obviously I was staggered and taken aback at the same time and my sister was equally shocked. I knew this because as my head swiveled and I began to see stars she let out a little squeal. I am not completely certain as I was a bit dazed but it sounded like the sound, "Oowee" came out of my mouth.

At the time this occurred Nina was already on her top bunk and the look on her face said, *"Did my Momma just slap my sister in the face?"* Meanwhile I stood there with my face stinging like I was doing the nature dance in the middle of a beehive. I don't even recall taking the time to cry I just stood there like a mannequin posed with a look of astonishment. As if to add insult to injury, Momma then blurted out, *"I slapped you once and I'll slap you twice if you don't shut this mess up and go to bed now!"* That was a phrase that my sister and I joked about for years following that incident. We would creep up behind Momma and try to imitate her voice, *"I slapped you once and I'll slap you twice..."* then we would all burst out laughing. That was the only time that Momma ever laid a hand on me. Sometimes I do wish she had been a little tougher on us but I know that her gentle spirit would not allow her to be. I laugh about it now because it is the most entertaining memories I have of my older sister and my Momma, both whom have passed away. It is in such a vulnerable moment of introspection, that I understand the medicinal nature of humor. It also clarifies for me the reason why comedians seem to be able to make people laugh because they can incorporate things from their past or family happenings. They often take painful and dramatic experiences and give them a twist. For many the humor is a means of entertaining while simultaneously keeping them from "losing their minds."

Momma had an unshakeable faith and always believed that God would see us through. Wanting to give us the same foundation of faith that she enjoyed, we were carted promptly and dutifully to church from an early age. This was following in the religious tradition of our cultural heritage. This was also supported by the biblical instruction to *"train up a child in the way that he or she should go and when they are old they will not depart from it."* That truth not only rang true for me but ultimately it produced a family tradition. Continuing in that long standing tradition, I also took my children to church.

Now don't be mistaken into thinking that we were some kind of *lovey, dovey,* kind of family. We were not always touchy or feely, but when Momma hugged, you knew it was genuine. Although I can't ever remember her wearing a special perfume, I believe that her scent was sweet if for no other reason simply because of whom she was and her treatment of people. She was patient and understanding, and very accepting of an individual's faults. Although I did not have a Father's love, I had the love of my Momma and she was truly my heaven and my earth.

One song that Momma loved more than any other song in this world was the gospel song, *His Eye is on the Sparrow.* Her love and passion for gospel music as a genre categorically was tremendous. When she became ill, gospel music is what Dora would constantly play for her to comfort and soothe her soul. As technology evolved Momma became hooked on a new technological format, gospel videos. I'll never forget the last time I went to see her at home before she went one final time to the hospital. I can still visualize her sitting in her wheelchair, wrapped like an Eskimo in her parka and blankets. She was transfixed like little Ronnie Jr., that night in the bedroom, gazing intently at the television set. Only instead of watching images of a Grandpa she was watching, you probably guessed it gospel videos. I tried to turn the channel. Stupid me. She quickly said in a very weak but audible voice, *"no baby that's what Momma wants to hear, leave it there."*

Instinctually I knew at that exact moment, she was soon going to pass; she was going home to the other side, to heaven. Silent and contemplative, I drove home while gospel music sifted through the speakers, my apposite companion. All the while I was thinking about Momma. Momentarily pausing, I silently petitioned God, *"Lord please allow her to stay just a little while longer."* One thing that is for certain when he calls you home it is just your time to go, and that's all there is to it. And this was Momma's moment to exit stage left. Taking her final bow to a thunderous applause from a grateful people, Momma passed into her eternal life. She joined the Heavenly Gospel Choir, on December 22nd, 2003. Sometimes I think I can almost hear her distinct song-bird voice echoing the lyrics of *His Eye is on the Sparrow*, when the night is still.

Although my Momma was probably the most important person in my life, there yet remained seasons in which I yearned for a Father's love. It was not just the love that he could give but also the security and strength that only a man can give. I think most of all I wanted him so desperately to simply acknowledge that I was his. In doing so it would have validated and added a measure of security to me as a child.

Security to a child again cannot be overstated. One of the times in my life when I truly needed to feel secure, wrapped in a Father's Love, was when I first thought my brother and sister were going to be taken from me. I just knew they were going to be whisked away from Dora and put in foster care, or so we thought. This period of fear and uncertainty concerning our shared future followed a custody battle between my younger brother's father and my mother, Dora. His father had accused our mother of being an unfit parent. Following that accusation, a petition was filed with the County Welfare Agency office. During this lengthy ordeal we were terrified that we were going to be split up and possibly never see one another again. My grandmother (Momma) was the one that stepped in and began to get involved in the legal custody process with her daughter during this period.

Eventually a court date was scheduled; Dora and Momma had to attend the hearing. This hearing was for the purpose of determining whether or not Dora was mentally fit to be a parent. It would also answer the questions of whether or not my brother's father would gain custody of him and whether the rest of us would be placed in foster care by the County Welfare Agency. As siblings who drew strength and courage from each other we were apprehensive of the outcome. I remember us huddling together on the couch crying and simultaneously praying to God that we would not be split up. Our separation anxiety was further reinforced by the fact that previously my older brother's father had already been awarded custody of him. Against the backdrop of this heart wrenching court saga I reflected again on my father. If ever there was a time that I so desperately needed a fathers love and protection, it was once again, here and now.

Suddenly outside the apartment where we were waiting, our fears were briefly interrupted by the sound of a car pulling up to the residence. It seemed like an eternity before we heard the faint but distinct closing of the car door and the shuffling of shoes, clicking up the driveway. Muscles became tense and the grip that we had upon one another became tighter. My eyes felt like they could pop out of the sockets at any moment. Would this be the end of my proverbial world or would this be another twist in a life of recurrent new beginnings? *"Oh God Please..."* I silently prayed, just in case he did not hear my previous requests. Suddenly the hero stepped onto the stage and the audience could breathe a sigh of relief. You know those trumpet sounds and the upbeat music that's heard right as the hero comes to the rescue? In that moment of inexplicable joy and immeasurable satisfaction I experienced the euphoria of being rescued.

Why? Because in walks Momma followed by Dora, emerging from the taxi alone, we were so relieved. Just to make sure they were not being followed I kept straining my little eyes hoping to further confirm what I was seeing. There were no paparazzi, no flashing lights, and no child care workers, not one. Convinced at last I begin to think about the possibility of authentic hope and of new beginnings. Relief was a power so real and so sweet that I could feel the tension that previously held my body captive beginning to subside. It melted like snow and trickled away off the side of *Fears Mountain*. First the tension in my head, then shoulders, down to my stomach, and out through my toes.

Then finally we were a typhoon of giddy child-like energy again. Bouncing on the couch so hard and so fast I thought in a moment the springs might pop their wiry heads out and tear through the fabric. But just as quickly as that joy emerged Momma sat down to explain to us what had happened. Sensing the importance of this moment as it related to our future we too begin to once again compose ourselves. Finally as the room hushed she spoke, *"Children..."*she began *"because of..."* she paused again *"your mother's problems, I have been given sole custody of you all. That is at least until she is once again able to get herself together, and get back on her feet."* Although we could not understand exactly what she was talking about all I knew was that we were going to remain together, and her sacrifice warmed my heart and sent a fuzzy chill down my spine.

Even today I thank God for that promise that Momma made to take care of us while Dora worked on her life issues. There are going to be circumstances where a parent cannot take care of a child, and that's just one of the many facts of life. It is however liberating to know that there are God sent surrogates who are willing to step in. This was our story and this is the story of millions of children around the world, not just in America. The power of that promise will remain embedded in the lives of children for as long as they are breathing. No child will forget the sacrifices that are made for them. They may have short term memory loss and rebel during particular seasons of life but in terms of the power of a promise, and the follow through, its redemptive power has no equal. It always has and always will be the most powerful means of shaping and molding a child into a person of wholeness and one who can duplicate the acts of service received when they were young.

Momma's strength, courage and determination were what kept me going as a child. From my biological parents I inherited genes and chromosomes. From Momma I inherited the intangible life lessons and associated character development, tools that ultimately shaped me as a person. It was as I witnessed the strength and perseverance she displayed in moments such as the court hearing. Her conscious decision and commitment to raise us, was a sacrificial choice to ensure that we would be more productive and healthy citizens of the world at large. What an amazing gift she gave us, and what an amazing opportunity that many caring adults will have to give to children all over the world. May this story move you to *reflection*, to *conviction*, and hopefully stir you to *action*. In addition to strength and perseverance, I gained a sense of wholeness and balance, a desire to be affectionate. These attributes were not just observed from her occasionally but she was consistent in application. That is a great moral victory that has defined who I have become today. Although it may sound dramatic in essence I owe Momma my life, although I wish I had such strong conviction for my biological father it didn't turn out that way. Maybe it was just not meant to be.

What of Momma's Social life? One word can describe that aspect, non-existent. Not only did Momma not have a social life she did not even have many male companions with which to share companionship. The two male companions that I can remember were very abusive men and therefore the memory of such leaves behind a residue; a grapefruit like bitter taste in one's mouth. I can remember coming home one day from school and hearing screams echoing off the walls of the house, as I approached. As I ran fearfully up the front porch steps, through the windows I could see Momma's boyfriend Calvin beating her in the face with his fist. It was like a scene from a horror flick, very graphic, very fast, and certainly surreal. Although numb and surrounded by feelings of helplessness I can remember screaming for Momma through the window. *"Momma, Momma...."* I wonder if she could hear me or even see me.

Then I tried banging on the window trying desperately to get her attention. Finally exasperated and with a frantic lunge I began pulling on the door. My little body rocked back and forth yanking on the handle but this ultimately proved to be a fruitless endeavor. The door was locked and there was no way that I was getting in, at least not that way. Then with the sounds of my Momma's screams now echoing of the walls of my very being I went to the back window of the duplex hoping to get a better view. Instead the horror reel just got more graphic as I saw Momma's face now bloody and battered from unyielding merciless fists. This hue of rainbow colors that now berated my psyche was too much. It was the final straw for me. I now understand what gives people the strength to do the impossible in that moment of truth. It is part fear, mixed with desperation, and a deep sense that something must happen and it must happen now! With that feeling I turned and saw a brick lying on the ground. It's funny how you notice certain things exactly at the moment that you need them. Crouching quickly down like a princess warrior I scooped it up, reached my arm back like a major league pitcher and threw it forward with all my force. The shattering of the glass opened a hole in the center of the window but there were still sharp shards of glass that outlined the outside frame of the window. Still in princess warrior mode I used my fist to knock out the remaining glass just enough so that I could wiggle my way through. My heart raced and my adrenaline was exploding but at that moment all the pain seemed meaningless. The superfluous picture image of Momma being beat by this gorilla like beast of a man was more than my little heart could bare.

Calvin, never even seemed to notice the commotion, he just kept on pummeling Momma. It is as though his rational mind had shut down and he was mechanically releasing some anger that had been pent up for years. Momma's screams were tearing through my little heart now like a tiger's paws on the side walls of a deer that was soon to become its next meal. I did not have a plan for what I would do next all I knew is that I had to separate this man from Momma. Where was my Father? Where was my Mother? Where was anybody to assist me with helping her? Then I found my voice. *"Leave my Momma alone!"* I screamed at the gorilla man. By this time Momma's strength was subsiding as I witnessed her body weakening under the onslaught of this abuse. The cruel twist of fate was here stood a woman who fought so hard to save our lives, fighting for the continuance of her very own life. It was just too cruel and too warped for words.

I knew that if I did not intercede immediately she would most likely not make it because she was losing the battle badly. Then I remember that we kept a baseball bat behind the door. I hastily sprang towards it, grabbed it and started swinging as hard as I could towards Calvin. While swinging the bat I continued to yell at him, *"Get off my Momma and to leave her alone!"* This possessed man seemed intent upon doing no less than killing my Momma. Although I was swinging the bat with everything I had I realized that the blunt impact was not fazing him. Being a child of moderate weight and build I saw the bat bouncing off him as if it was made of rubber. *"This is just not fair"*, I silently thought. I could feel my body growing more exhausted and the adrenaline that had been so powerful now decreased considerably.

 But then something amazing happened. One of blows of the bat struck Calvin in the head, squarely causing him to reel in pain. Suddenly he was jerked forcefully back into reality. Sensing the danger Momma screamed at me, *"Run Reese, run baby!"* I turned and darted like a rabbit to the left and then to the right scarcely evading Calvin's frantic grasp. I can only imagine based upon what he did to Momma what he would have done to me. Even now I shudder to think about it. Calvin must have been drunk. His reflexes were slowed considerably and he seemed to half stumble half lunge towards me. By now the horror flick is moving at a frantic pace. It is that scene where the protagonist is desperately trying to avoid the antagonist and the audience sits pinned to the edge of their seats cheering the protagonist on. Oh, don't act like you don't scream just as loudly hoping to somehow aid the actor or actress in their difficult escape. By now I'm moving quickly toward the door and as Momma's yelling at me to run, I am yelling at her to run as well. Then I told her she should call the police. It was a truly terrifying ordeal. The police finally arrived and Calvin was promptly jailed on battery charges. While they were booking him and preparing to whisk him away I began the delicate and gruesome task of cleaning up Momma's face. When Dora came home a couple of days later we told her what Calvin had done. Upon Calvin's release from jail Dora and her friends dealt with him swiftly and decisively. I know this must be true because after that he never came near my Momma again.

As a child unfortunately this experience was not an isolated event. I frequently saw this type of abuse inflicted on both my Momma and Dora as well. This coupled with my Father's abandonment and rejection of me, increased my distrust of men. As a result I became not only afraid of men when I was young but it also carried over into my teenage years as well. It impacted me emotionally in that sense, and also psychologically in terms of finding wholeness. Not having a Father's Love meant that part of my inner self was missing. In many faith traditions and religious organizations, there is a philosophy that the Father has an endowment that is to be imparted into each child. Without that endowment there was a disconnection between the person I was and who I felt inside that I *should* be. In other words I didn't fully understand what my purpose as a young woman was supposed to be. Therefore I am convinced the unfulfillment of a promise, in a child's life is something that will hinder the establishment of their self identity. I believe that many of the young men and women who make poor choices in life do so out of an awareness of that lack, that endowment. They draw the conclusion that they must not be worthy of your promise and therefore decide to live somewhat recklessly. It is a story as old as time itself, that continues to play over and over and over again, like the Movie "Ground Hog Day."

Make a decision today, Fathers, to release that endowment to each one of your children. If there are issues that you need to first deal with in your own life then make that a priority. It is not in the attainment of reciprocated and repetitive, physical and emotional escapades with women that you gain accomplishment. Rather, it is in the bonding with your children and the fulfillment of your God pre-ordained purpose for their lives. Promise to complete that pre-established mission, to the best of your ability. And in doing so, God will promise and fulfill the destined purpose in your own life.

TIP 2: *Never make a promise you cannot keep:* Children are so vulnerable and trusting that they tend to hang onto their parents every word. In many ways especially while they are young you become such an integral part of their world. That is why they often follow you around even when you would much rather spend time alone. Knowing the impact of your words make sure to evaluate what promises you actually will be able to keep before you commit to your child. Otherwise they will nag you until you either yield or break. For many this results in you yelling out of frustration, both at them for expecting completion, and simultaneously at yourself for not fulfilling your stated promise. How many kids are walking around today with spirit's that are still crushed from promises that never materialized? Probably a more important question is, *"Are yours?"*

Chapter 3: My Family Circle of Women

The Perfect Stranger

Do you remember me?

How could you forget the day we first met?

And I slept in your arms till dawn

Do you remember my first bike ride?

How many times I tried

How you held on to be my guide

Do you remember my first day of school, or my skinned knee?

Do you even remember me?

You missed the chance to chase the boys away

The chance to tell me you loved me everyday

You missed the chance to tell me to be good

To always do the things a real lady should

One thing you missed worth more than any million-dollar prize

Is you missed the chance to look into your daughters eyes

ShaRhonda

*I*n my own family the existence of "father-daughter relationships" was not especially common. As matter of fact of the five girls that my mother had, only my older sister enjoyed a relationship with her father. I have seen countless women who have been abused by men, including my sisters. Their syndrome was known as **(LOFI)** *"lack-of-Father-itis"*. This is not an official medically recognized term but one that I created myself. I coined this term to express a need to have a male father figure who can help them, protect them, and love them. When they don't find this ultimately they settle for substitutes. For many children, especially young daughters they find themselves on an endless life-long quest, for love. They are always searching but never quite finding a man that will love and respect them and ultimately fulfill their needs.

Why do they look for fulfillment in others, particularly men, you ask? Some women have a hard time loving themselves because again as stated previously in the book because they experienced childhood abandonment, they are not worthy of love. To further complicate the matter there are men who will lurk, searching for easy prey. These men promptly recognize women who display symptoms of **LOFI** and ultimately try to ensnare them. As unhealthy as it may appear to an outsider these same women will stay in an abusive relationship simply because they conclude that *any* love is better than *no* love. You might hear such a woman argue, *"Girl, he don't mean no harm sometimes I just get him upset and that's just the way my man is."* To try to convince such a woman to leave a relationship is often a fruitless endeavor.

Ultimately they must draw that conclusion on their own, that they deserve better. That does not mean that if you know someone in an abusive relationship you should not offer support, it is simply to forewarn you of the challenges you will face. In regards to my own family circle of women, I would often wonder why they allowed such abuse and did not fight back. Sometimes as demented or bizarre as the logic may seem, women may feel that any attention from a man is equated with love. My reaction to seeing this unhealthy generational pattern among my female family members was to determine that I would break the cycle. No matter what I told myself, I will accept nothing less than complete respect from a man.

It is an empowering moment ladies when you finally have the conviction and intuitiveness to determine that you will accept nothing less than total respect for yourself and therefore not allow abuse. If a man shows symptoms of abuse at the beginning of the relationship what makes you think that he is going to change? Well the next question then should be what are some of the symptoms or warning signs? I submit to you the following. Let's say that he is controlling, suspicious of your activities, jealous, and short tempered, then those are early warning signs. Avoid such a man at all cost and if possible encourage him to seek counseling for his anger issues. If not then you will risk becoming a statistic like so many women in my family unfortunately have.

What does that do psychologically to your children when they see this? For girls it teaches them that abuse is ok and they are more inclined to allow it because mommy was ok with it. Even for young men who witness abuse, they feel as though it is ok to abuse women that they date. Instead of learning to deal with their anger in healthy and responsible ways, they become *"gorilla men"* themselves. In my opinion a *"gorilla man"* is someone who rather than operate by fundamental principles that are based on human decency, he instead becomes a Calvin. Becoming intoxicated or hooked on drugs, or any other vice does not excuse abuse either. The person that you were before you indulged in those vices is simply magnified by the drugs and alcohol. It simply causes you to feel a greater sense of ease to do what internally you have wanted to do anyway. For those good men out there that don't abuse women my hat goes off to you and we applaud your efforts, continue in that tradition because *"innocent eyes"* are watching you.

My Momma's abusive relationships started many years back. She remembers being in one abusive relationship after another. When she married my grandfather life was no different. He not only had the reputation of being an abuser but he was also a womanizer and an alcoholic. Someone with those attributes does not make a good partner. Momma said he beat her constantly and therefore he was no different than the men abusers before him. When she became pregnant with Dora, she figured that the abuse would stop. Unfortunately this was not the case it simply continued. After Dora was born, Momma again became pregnant and was soon to conceive.

During the second pregnancy my grandfather beat Momma so badly he ended up pushing her down the stairs in a drunken rage causing her to lose the baby.

Fearing for the life of Dora and herself Momma eventually left my grandfather. Momma left Dora, with her in-laws since she had no resources to care for her. Also, due to the extremity of the abuse she had been dealing with, Momma felt it would be the best way for her to get her life back on track. It was a difficult decision but Momma knew that Dora would be in safe and loving hands with her grandparents, and that contact could be sustained. Dora said she never really knew her biological father, due to the fact he was never around. At one point in her life she recalls hearing through the grapevine that he was in jail. The void of a missing father was filled by her step-grandfather instead. Even still I know that Dora dealt with the emotional baggage left from the residue of her tattered childhood. In my assessment of the situation, she was never able to gain completeness as a person due to the lack of Fatherly affection. Not to excuse the unhealthy patterns that existed for the women in my family but I understand to a greater degree why it was so difficult for Dora to give me what she never had, unconditional love. Especially, since a model of that unreserved love never came from her father.

Feeling incomplete and searching for a vice to fill the aching emptiness left by the void, Dora turned to drugs and alcohol. This battle and untimely addiction, led her down a spiral pathway that eventually led her into the arms of abusive men. Subconsciously as I mentioned earlier children tend to emulate their parents. I suppose that Dora figured if abusive relationships were ok for Momma then they were ok for her.

I can only recall meeting my paternal grandfather once or twice in my life. One fact about his life that is clear is that he died in the early 1970's of lung cancer. Missing the opportunity to get to know my grandfather was also a source of pain for me. I could never understand why as women we did not have strong male role models, to look up to or be close to in our family. I looked at the relationships that my mother, grandmother, and sisters had with men and I vowed never to duplicate the pattern of abusive relationships. As a defense mechanism I built a wall of security around myself as a child that remained well into my teenage years. Maintaining control of my environment was a top priority and this included keeping boys at a distance. My deep rooted fear was that I would be hurt and abandoned like I was during childhood by my father.

The one of the few men that I can truly say made an impact on my life as a child was my step-grandfather. He and my great grandmother would always come to visit us from time to time. They always knew the right times to come. That was mostly at the end of the month when food was running low and we needed extra help to make ends meet. The second man who came into my life as a child and who made a great impact on my life was my great uncle, Momma's brother. I first met Uncle Ernest, Aunt Augusta and my first cousins when I was approximately 8 or 9 years old. I knew Momma had a sister because we would visit my Aunt Jewel often. During the course of my childhood there were periods where she only lived a few blocks from us. It did however come as a surprise to us that Momma had a brother. This was due to the fact she never talked about him or his wife. Having them in addition to Aunt Jewel, Uncle Ernest, and my cousins made life all the more sweeter.

I don't think my mother Dora ever fully understood her children, and I was no exception. It seemed like Dora often resented having children and often avoided being around us. I assumed that was why she stayed in the streets so much when we were young. Maybe it was because she started having children at the tender age of 15. When you are a child yourself how can you begin to understand the needs of a helpless baby? It seemed to me that she was always troubled, searching for something. Maybe she was running away from life, kids, responsibilities. Maybe she was running from herself or in her mind to herself. Who knows?

In terms of physical features my mother was an attractive woman. Each one of us, as her daughters, got our physical features from her. Some of those features included brown skin, and a beautiful smile. Especially our smile and we were always fashionably dressed, just like our mother. Dora was always trendily dressed. Oh yes! My mother loved clothes, shoes, and she had to have her hair and makeup just right. Also, she took care of her skin which complemented the fact that she aged well. Dora was a Gemini; some often refer to Gemini's as having *"two heads"*. This was almost like a self fulfilling prophecy that manifested in her having a split personality, almost bi-polar tendencies. One minute she was Dr Jekyll and the next minute Mr. Hyde. In addition, she wasn't a people's person, which made her not only unpredictable, but anti-social. Although she did have casual friends she would never let anyone of them get close to her, this included her kids.

Dora choosing to be distant from us as her children was a complex reality that I struggled to come to terms with. In my opinion why have children if you don't want to raise and nurture them? I suppose that just like I put a wall up, to avoid being further abused by men she responded in similar fashion. It had to be a difficult position compounded by the fact that she did not know her biological father; her children had several different fathers, and other men that moved in and out of her life like a revolving door to contend with. Although she chose to be distant from us she still made sure that Momma had all the resources she needed to keep the house going. Dora always made sure there was food in the house even if it did not last until the end of the month. Even though it may not have been the Ritz Carton we always had a roof over our head. And even if it was only imitation *Ralph Lauren* or *Ed Hardy*, we always had clothes on our backs. Just kidding, they were not even imitation *fashion-wear*, they were usually hand me downs or clothes from the local thrift store!

TIP 3: *Shower your children with "I love you's"*: The words, "I love you" are music to your child's ear. They are three words that when combined together are more melodious than the greatest symphony ever played. The words also imply that you value your child and will be there with them through the ups and downs of life.

Chapter 4: Uncle Ernest and Visits to Michigan

Surrogate

You saw me in my greatest need

You cared for me like biological seed

A surrogate

When my world was dark, pain overwhelmed

"Magic Man" you sprinkled loves spell

My surrogate

Surrogate is as surrogate does

Surrogate was not obliged just because

The love you knew I craved and yearned

And the angel of light pricked your heart

To burn

As years go by I shan't forget

My prince of faith

My surrogate

I say as years go by I won't forget

You prince of faith

My....

Surrogate

Rudo

I will preface this chapter by pointing out the fact that although my Uncle Ernest resided in the State of Michigan, he was born in Ohio. This would make him a Buckeye to the core and he would recite this fact anytime the mention of "living in Michigan" was a conversation piece. When watching ESPN or the local sports channel, he always rooted for The Ohio State Buckeyes regardless of the sport.

When I try to recall events of my early childhood there are specific facts that remain blurry. The realization of such is indeed a strange phenomenon. I suppose that when I put up that internal wall specific, vivid images became buried deep inside the crevices of my subconscious. Like bones in the grave, long forgotten, some memories unfortunately will never return. The bones represent memories that are gut wrenching once uncovered. In the midst of that pain I was fortunate to have someone from whom I could gain hope and healing. That source of hope and healing was my Great Uncle Ernest.

I think I fell in love with him the moment he stepped though our front door. I can't fully explain the instant attraction. Maybe it had something to do with the fact he noticed me and also acknowledged what I was doing at the time. In retrospect it was a great surprise to me, that a man would take such notice

My Uncle Ernest was your typical, *D & H*, dark and handsome Black man. Not only did he *have* these stunningly amazing attributes but he *knew* he looked good. He stood somewhere between 5"9" and 6"0" tall with broad shoulders. He was the total package. His aura and presence so transformed a room that when he entered women's head's would swivel like a bobble doll. Even before he entered a room, his booming voice introduced him long before you ever saw him. By the looks of him I concluded that he didn't take any mess. Not only that he struck me as someone who was opinionated and didn't mind sharing that opinion with others.

 Ah yes, and of course he had to have a trademark outfit right? His was more of an accessory fetish, consisting of fishing hats or a stunning fedora. He knew that he could pretty much wear any hat, actually. As he got older his style in accessories, hats to be more specific evolved. He was more into a laid back style that included baseball caps. As you can probably figure out, the OSU emblem was proudly displayed on any sports hat that he donned. As I mentioned earlier living in Michigan did not diminish The Ohio State Buckeye blood that pulsated through every vein in his body. Later when I married an Ohio State Basketball player, that decision was almost certainly the coronation in his cap.

Did I mention the fact that he was funny? Uncle Ernest had a bagful of sayings that he could just whip out during any occasion. One of his

favorite sayings was from the late 70's/80's sitcom, Stanford and
Son's. He would call you a *"Big Dummy,"* in a minute which sounds
shocking to someone unaware of his personality. In fact it was really
just a term of endearment that meant he liked and even loved you.
My children had to get used to that because they actually thought he
was serious when he called them, *"ya big dummy!"* I had to constantly
remind them that he was only joking with them and not intending the
phrase literally. After a period of adjustment they began to
understand and would laugh whenever he would say it. When I
would to visit him sometimes I tried to beat him to the punch. Upon
opening the door I might greet him by saying, *"Hey ya Big dummy how
ya doing?"* Since I was obviously connecting with him in a way that he
understood he got a huge kick out of it. After appearing momentarily
taken aback, a huge grin would spread across his face and he would
grab me in a mighty bear hug. His response would be, *"I'm fine now
that you are here."* And that was just how my Uncle Ernest was.

He and I shared a bond like none other. Notwithstanding my
wedding day and the birth of my four children, meeting Uncle Ernest
was one of the best moments of my life. Since as a child I had no
father the bond with Uncle Ernest was like a queen meeting her
modern day king and protector for life. It now makes more sense to
me the importance or symbolism of a Father giving his daughter
away at a wedding. In essence it is a Father saying to another man, I
have protected and cared for my daughter in my household for many
years. Now she leaves my care and protection and you become her
husband and king.

The day I first met Uncle Ernest I had been ironing everyone's clothes like I always did. This was my assigned chore and gave me the opportunity to help out around the house. Since Momma took care of and sacrificed for us I felt it was the least I could do. Well anyway, all of a sudden my daily routine was interrupted by a loud knock at the door. You can always tell the difference between a timid knock and the knock of someone who is exceptionally sure about themselves. Uncle Ernest was the latter and that confident knock was followed by a loud manly voice, *"Ruby...Ruby is anyone home?"* That was followed by the brisk steps of my Momma heading towards the door. She must have let him in because the next thing I know I am staring up at this man who notices how hard at work I am ironing those clothes.

Maybe it was because he mistakenly thought I was Cinderella, living under the evil forces of a tyrant old stepmother. Who knows? What I do know is that from that moment on, he had a soft spot in his heart for me. I recall Momma's face lighting up when she saw him. I did not even know my Grandmother had a brother, because she never spoke about him. When she first introduced us, *"...this is your Uncle Ernest,"* needless to say, I was surprised. He followed the introduction by asking Momma, *"Why do you have an 8 year old ironing a large basketful of clothes?"* My Momma's reply was non-verbal as she simply stared at him with wide eyes like she had seen a ghost. Perhaps she had no response to this abrupt and direct question. In my mind however, it was no big deal, because this was what I always did.

This was just one example of a man who was not only loud and boisterous but always seemed to get what he wanted. I had never met anyone like him before and was very fascinated. He did not travel alone he brought along another gentleman, and his oldest son Tim, my cousin. After the formalities were behind us Uncle Ernest turned and asked me, *"where is the nearest store?"* After getting the location and directions, he took my sister Anna and I with him around the corner to the store. He told us the seven magic words that are sure to spoil any child, *"You can get anything that you want."* Anna and I first looked in amazement at each other, our eyes as big as two saucers after spotting a mars spaceship land on planet earth. Then we turned and looked at Momma and Cousin Tim just to confirm the news that we had just received. Both just casually nodded as if to say, *"go ahead its* ok *if Uncle Ernest say's it is".* Now to some kids this may not be a big deal but to us this was huge. There was never any extra money in our house for splurging and spending like this. Knowing how hard she worked and penny pinched, we knew not to even ask Momma. In fact we were just glad to have a roof over our head and clothes on our backs.

Anna and Tim chose some chips and soda and it seemed to take them a relatively short period of time to make up their minds. In contrast I wanted to relish this experience and strolled down every aisle looking for the perfect gift. All of a sudden I spotted it. The gift that was what I had been looking for. It was right near the entrance when we first walked into the store. It was a ceramic tea set and I thought it would be a charming gift that would bring many blissful memories. The set had little teacups, saucers, and even had a teapot for pouring. I guess the reason that I liked it was that it symbolized a special moment in time in my life. Someone was actually buying me a gift, or cared about what I wanted.

Even if I never saw Uncle Ernest or Cousin Tim again, at least I would always have something special to remember them by. And for a little girl that ached so desperately for a Father's love, this man was someone that at that moment was providing things that I needed to fill that void. Not so much the gift, although it was indeed nice, but the empathy and kindness that he displayed was multi-faceted. My Uncle Ernest was a bit surprised at my choice and asked, *"Are you sure you don't want candy, soda, or something to snack on?"* I nodded emphatically that I didn't, "No I want the tea set please," I insisted. Of course he purchased it and I remember holding onto that tea set for many years after our first meeting.

After that all of us Momma, Uncle Ernest, Anna, Tim, and me chatted casually and laughed often. In the midst of our conversation my Uncle as is his trademark way blurted out, *"I am taking Reese back to Michigan with me, when I leave!"* He said it so emphatically and in such a matter of fact way that it was almost like it was already decided. I began to feel the jitters, a mixture of excitement and apprehension all bundled up together. I had never been outside the State of Ohio before and therefore did not know what to anticipate. Of course not wanting me too far out of her sight Momma said just as emphatically, *"No she can't go."* Uncle Ernest shot right back, *"Why it's not like she is needed here, not to mention the fact its summer time. What's more kids need a vacation every once in a while and while the rest of you are working, this girl could use some fun!"*

Even though I had the jitters and was not even sure if I wanted to go this back and forth debate between Momma and Uncle Ernest was like a high profile legal case proceeding. I wondered who would ultimately win the contest. After a spirited back and forth conversation Momma finally conceded and I remember everyone started to cry as the reality of me going away became more palpable. Even though it was not the same thing my mind briefly flashed back to the memory of the day Momma went to court to gain custody of us. Here again even if temporarily the ambiguity of my living arrangements was thrust at the forefront of my life. My uneasiness began to build as Momma and Anna helped me pack my suitcase. When it was finally time to go I realized that I was torn inside. On the one hand, Momma was my safe haven and I could not imagine leaving her. On the other hand I privately wanted to go with my Uncle perhaps curiosity and the chance to take a much needed voyage was gradually becoming intriguing. When I had finally settled in the back seat with my cousin Tim the finality of it hit me, I was actually going. Tears began to well up in my eyes as the car pulled away from the house. I waved bravely to my Momma and my sister Anna trying to imagine what thoughts were presently going through their minds. Maybe Momma was panicking wondering if I had remembered to take everything that I needed. I am sure she also fretted over whether or not she had made the right decision. Anna probably was overcome with mixed emotions of excitement and sadness simultaneously. I am sure that like me she was sad that we would not hang out during the summer, like we had in the past. Happy, because that meant that she would have more space and special treatment from Momma since I would be gone. There were so many questions that were swimming around inside my head. *"Where is Michigan anyway?" "Is it far?"* I wondered how long it would take for us to get there. Of course I did not dare to ask these questions out loud. I was too nervous and plus this was the first man I had ever been around aside from my Grandfather that I would be seeing this summer on a regular basis.

As I suspected the drive was indeed a long one. In fact it was a little too long for me if you really want to know. I remember seeing so much water outside my window, it seemed like it was everywhere I turned. Years later when I traveled those roads with my children they would play *the water game* that their cousins taught them. These lessons occurred when they were on the way to Ohio for their first trip. The object of one of the games is for you to be the first to spot the lakes or puddles you saw before reaching your destination. The person who claimed the highest number of bodies of water when we arrived was the winner of the game. The way to claim a body of water is indeed an unusual one. Shouting *"That's my water!"* before anyone else would add to your bounty. And such a statement would garner one point. I am sure that for the driver the sound of kids shouting continuously in the back of the car was like nails scratching a blackboard. Hey, at least you wouldn't have to worry about falling asleep at the wheel right?

I remember lots of open fields passing by like a blur. As the day transformed into night I began to feel homesick, and missed Momma. By now, my little body was contorted in the smallest possible corner of the back seat. My Uncle Ernest and Cousin Tim sensing my growing anxiety quietly but firmly assured me that everything would be fine and that we were almost there. I must admit that even though I was in a strange place I did get excited when I saw a sign that said **Michigan Welcomes' You**. Given the fact that this signaled I was almost there, I would look for this sign on all my future trips to Michigan to see my Uncle, Aunt and cousins. Not only did I always look for the Michigan sign, I shared with my children the significance of the sign. They too would look for the sign as we traveled and upon spotting it scream, *"We are almost in Michigan!"*

When we finally arrived at the house I could not believe how gigantic the house was. It looked like one of those mansions that you see in a movie, the reality show *"Cribs"*, or in a glamour magazine to me. Of course part of this perspective had to do with the fact that I lived in the projects back home. The house had a huge tree in the front yard and the property was fenced in. The fenced front porch was of particular interest to me. I had never seen this accessory attached to a house before. I would spend many summer days and even holidays, thereafter sitting on that front porch. I remember my Uncle, Auntie, cousins and I would watch television, visit with friends, and truly bond over the years on that very porch.

Sometimes even as I slept indoors on the couch I could catch the cool breeze that came through the screens at night. Of course this was a real treat since the technology of centralized air had not become a reality yet. I was also very intrigued with the layout of the interior of the house. For instance you could actually go upstairs through two separate entrances either the kitchen or the family room. Again coming from the projects I thought that was extremely cool. I was so in love with that interior layout, I never forgave my Aunt when she remodeled her kitchen. This was because she ended up closing off one side, one entrance leading upstairs. She admitted later that she also regretted what she too described as a decoration gaffe.

My Aunt Augusta made me feel at ease from the moment I walked through her door. I must say that she was and still is the sweetest woman that I've ever met. She welcomed me in the house like it was a homecoming, as though she had known me for years. Meeting my other two cousins (Paula, and Anthony) that evening was also pleasant. I was informed by my Aunt that I would be sleeping in the same room as them. From the moment we were introduced that evening I remember the three of us staying up chatting and laughing, all night. It was a great opportunity for the three of us to get to know each other. Eventually I suppose our exuberance and excitement reached an extremely high volume level. Aunt Augusta came in the room and told us firmly but politely, *"Children it is time to go to sleep now."*

Over the years her strong conviction and value of family and God influenced and helped mold me into the woman that I am today. To use a biblical figure, she had the patience of Job, and then some. I scratch my head even now and don't know how she was able to deal with all that she dealt with. The bond shared with my Aunt, Uncle and cousins was like nothing else that I have known. I think that is why I kept going back summer after summer. I wanted to experience the comradery and reconnection experienced with family and friends. They truly made my heart full of love. It was during those periods that I was probably able to best deal with the loss from not having the love of a Father. I also knew that when I had children I wanted them to have this same sense of connection, affection and bonding with family.

In terms of male role models my Uncle Ernest was the second male to come into my life and impact me in a positive way. The first of course was my step-grandfather, whom I called Uncle George. I guess it just sounded better than *"Step-Grandfather dude"*. Over the years I appreciated them both. In particular my love for Uncle Ernest intensified due to the summer periods that we would spend together. Those couple of weeks during each summer gave me a chance to break from the monotonous rigors of life in the projects.

TIP 4: *Give lots of praise and encouragement*: Children love praise. As matter of fact they thrive off of praise. Encouragement does wonders for a child's self esteem. Praise and encouragement builds up a child's overall sense of confidence and self worth. Encouraging words are like Vitamins; they feed the spirit and give your child that extra boost of nutrition needed for sustenance. Nutrition for the spirit will enable your child to overcome difficult obstacles and ultimately find success.

Chapter 5: Growing up Me

My Dad

I couldn't tell you how good my dad is to me

So I decided to write it in a poem to let you see

Whenever I need help he lends a helping hand

When I follow my dreams and fail

He's still my biggest fan

Me and my dad have a relationship so strong

People are not perfect but dad can do no wrong

How much I appreciate him

There aren't enough verses in a song

If it were, the song would be too long

He's my very own father and for that I am glad

Some people call him Mr. But I just call him my dad

Mariah

*M*y elementary years seemed like a blur to me. There are small segments of memory that I have retained in my subconscious mind, but not very many. Sometimes my general attitude is that life can be so unfair and disappointing. I have blocked out most of the memories of my younger years because they represent so much hurting. Kindergarten was a fun year in school however that I do remember. I recall my older brother had the responsibility of picking me up and walking me home from school. This as it turned out was not one of the highlights of his day although I could never understand why. I also loved my teacher that year. She was so young and vibrant and enjoyed teaching us, which made school fun. It made learning an enjoyable process for me.

One day in particular I remember wearing this beautiful party dress to school and these exquisite matching shoes that Dora had bought for me. I think I must have begged her to wear that specific dress that day because it was not a dress for school. I felt so beautiful that day as I attended classes. At the end of the day I was waiting for my brother as usual after school. All the other kids had gradually trickled off of the school yard either by bus, car, or foot. I kept thinking to myself *"where is my brother?"* Eventually I summed up the courage to convince myself that I could walk home by myself. I concluded that since I had walked with my brother on numerous occasions that it should be a piece of cake. I also began to imagine how proud Dora and Momma would be of me. The projects where we lived were not that far anyway, so if I left now I should be there shortly. Since my brother was taking so long to come I finally just started down the road. Girl gets tired of waiting for boy and leaves, typical strong willed girl for ya right?

When I finally made it home, Dora and Momma were both mortified and simultaneously relieved to see that I had made it home safe. I felt extreme vindication being left at the school and finding the courage to navigate my course instead of panicking. Come to think about it this was probably a symbolic moment that marked a distinct turning point. It symbolized one of the first times when I exhibited a willingness to trust my own instinct. I wanted both Momma and Dora to know that no matter what happened to me I could take care of myself.

Fast forwarding to the 5th -6th grade I had a much different experience. Perhaps this one was not one of my grandest moments but it lives on regardless. I remember one day at school getting in trouble for hitting a boy and causing his nose to bleed. In my humble opinion it was his fault to begin with. He kept taunting me and I remember on several occasions telling him to leave me alone. He wouldn't so I popped him hard in the nose. Of course as you can imagine I got in deep trouble with the teacher who reported it to the school administrative office. I do remember that the teacher asked me what caused me to hit the little boy. I responded, *"I forgot to eat my breakfast and I as a result I was agitated at myself. When he started taunting me it just sort of pushed me over the edge and he received the brunt of my frustration."*

For some unknown reason the teacher chose to turn the story around. The school contacted Dora and told her that I was very upset because she did not feed me breakfast and I was mad at my mother so I took it out on this poor boy. I was in trouble after that for sure. Dora said she could not believe what those people were telling her. To make matters worse she explained to me that the school could call the welfare office and they would come and take all of us away charging her with not feeding her children. She then asked me, *"Why would you tell your teacher that you are not getting fed?"* I tried to explain to Momma and Dora that the teacher had twisted my words, and give them my original statement but Dora would not believe me.

That day my faith in teachers was greatly diminished. I felt that they were not out to help me but to rather to hurt me. What compounded or further complicated the matter is the fact that in my opinion the majority of teachers looked down on me because I came from the projects. They could not see the potential that I had, only the environment that I came from. It brings up an important point often we overlook children or people simply based on their environment. We as human beings have a tendency to pre-judge people even though we may staunchly state that we don't.

Not only the fact that I was from the projects was a strike against me but there was more. My family was on welfare and there was no Father in the home. Having a Father's love would have been a welcomed luxury but I didn't even have a Father in the home. For the most part it was my Momma who raised me. So why should the school care anyway, was my attitude. I guess they figured if they never saw Dora at a parent teacher meeting then I would probably just end up a statistic anyway. As if this picture needed to get any bleaker, Momma could not drive. Amidst all of this difficulty and chaos, I had one saving Grace. I was somewhat smart in school. This was all the more unlikely not just given my family history of abuse and neglect but also my families educational background. Momma had a 6th grade education and Dora never finished the 10th grade. She was not around to help us with schoolwork anyway.

School was not always a drag though. There were enjoyable moments and I did take pleasure in being in school at times. School, like summers' spent with my Aunt and Uncle provided a break from the dysfunction of my everyday life. I was only an average student but I could have been a superior student if I had family support and had chosen to apply myself more. This would have been possible had I not been so busy just trying to survive and maintain my sanity. Along the way I did meet two teachers that I would classify as caring. The first whom I met in middle school sensed that my home life was not that great. She took me under her wing and gave me the encouragement that I needed to thrive and succeed. In high-school I met the other teacher who also was instrumental in promoting education and helping instill within me the will to thrive in school. Both teachers went above and beyond the call of duty when it came to mentoring me as a student. This special attention as I like to call it helped me to believe in myself. Both attended my high-school graduation and the presence of each one was vital. In actuality it was not just a victory for me but for the three of us as their role and sacrifice helped to make it possible.

Part of my internal drive to succeed was the fact that I did not want to end up on Welfare like my mother and grandmother. I did not want to become a victim of that family curse. The phrase, *"family curse"* applied in this context "is a pattern of behavior that reflects a families' dysfunction that is experienced generation after generation until it is finally broken." For my family it included poverty, drugs, welfare, alcoholism, and teenage pregnancy. What are the curses in your family? Knowing them and not accepting them as your pre-ordained destiny is the first step in overcoming and breaking the curse.

I'll never forget a Welfare caseworker saying to me, *"your Grandmother and Mother were both victims of welfare and you'll end up on welfare to."* These words fueled me to want to have a better life and to achieve a different level of success. Part of my success was completing my high-school education. I was determined not to allow anything to stand in my way. In my humble opinion, when I think about the Welfare system I feel it is probably the worst thing that was ever introduced to society. Notwithstanding the fact that it does provide general relief for families, but the long term affects on many families is devastating.

The Government cannot teach a person how to desire success. The Government cannot cause a person to want to get up in the morning and become a productive member of society. That desire has to come from a sense of shared value and a desire to have a better life. So in that sense the Welfare system has caused many families to become co-dependent on a system that is now dysfunctional. No one ever got rich by remaining on welfare. To summarize the importance of empowering and mobilizing people versus just giving them a handout I will refer back to the famous saying, *"If you give a man a fish he eats for a day, if you TEACH him to fish then he eats for a lifetime."* *(Unknown)*

I cannot begin to tell you how many houses that I have lived in growing up as a kid. Many of my friends have asked me to describe where I grew up and this is difficult given the fact there were so many locations. When asked to describe one place I would respond, *"Which hell hole do you want me to describe first?"* Still I can remember one house very vividly. It was so run down and out of code that it should have been condemned by the housing authority. I remember that we lived next to some train tracks and you would constantly hear the rumbling of passing trains and loud whistles blowing. You could always predict when the train was coming simply by watching the house. Specifically, the windows gave a warning they would shake in advance. This did not take place at a certain time of day but the trains ran 24 hours whether day or night. Furthermore, the house was so infested with roaches that it was even more of an extreme health hazard. To make it worse we had rats, yes rats that scurried continuously across our floor. The satire of the presence of rats was magnified by the fact that we also had wild cats living in the boarded up basement that we could not use.

The landlord, or should I say slumlord had the basement pad-locked. I was so afraid of being bitten by the rats and eaten by roaches I would constantly have nightmares. One time Momma was pressing my hair and a mother rat had dropped one of her babies in the middle of the kitchen floor. I totally freaked out. I just started screaming and hollering like I was going crazy. It scared Momma so bad that she dropped the hot comb that she was using to press my hair on my leg. She then jumped up to see what all the commotion was about. So now Momma is distressed because I was shocked by the rats, and to make matters worse my leg is on fire from the hot comb. I proceeded to fling the hot comb off of my leg and I started to cry uncontrollably. That night I was taken to the emergency room to be treated for second degree burns on my thigh. I still have remnants of the scar to this very day. Of course Momma felt horrible for the whole incident and I reassured her that it was not her fault.

I constantly suggested to Momma that the landlord should let the cats up from the basement to allow them to eat the rats. I believed this would not only solve the rat problem but it would also enable the food chain process, or the Circle of Life, to happen. Momma would just laugh at my suggestion. To my chagrin the landlord never did anything about the problem that we had with rodents and bugs. All he was concerned about was getting his rent money. He did not care about a single mother with five kids. He also was not motivated to improve the housing situation because he knew that my mother had nowhere else to go. As I shared before I lived many places, the projects, in a duplex house, in addition to an assortment of rented homes at one time or another.

One house that we lived in I actually did enjoy and I know that Dora did as well. I am not quite sure how she stumbled on it but it was nice. She lived upstairs and we lived downstairs with Momma. It was like living in two apartments stuck together that were squished together to formed a house. The house had a huge back yard with an apple, pear, and plum tree. We actually lived next door to my Aunt Jewel, Momma's baby sister. This was indeed my favorite house because I was allowed to keep a dog at the property. The dog was actually a mutt but he was my mutt and I did not care. I called him Coco because of his chocolate coat. Of course he had to stay outside, but I was just glad to have his companionship. Coco was my friend and I loved him and knew that he loved me as well. The house had a huge front and back porch, which was an addition we had not previously had in former housing arrangements. Therefore for us it seemed like a *step up*, no pun intended. We stayed in that house for many years.

TIP 5: *Create Memories and Traditions*: Create a legacy for your child. Something as simple as reading to them before bedtime is a powerful shared tradition. Other helpful ideas include having a special nickname, personal holiday, or family ritual that can be passed down. Remember the Michigan sign in the story? That became a shared memory that my children and I will recall for years to come. Don't overlook the simple things like playing board games, or going fishing. When you include them in these types of activities you create warm feelings that permeate their inner being. They feel like warm apple pie on the inside. Then when they experience difficult situations like the one that I experienced with my teacher that day they are ok. It is a hazard of life to have teachers, or outside figures that may not believe your children. Don't get mad about it and threaten to sue the school. Just prepare your children by creating supportive and esteem building moments at home.

Chapter 6: "Daddy"

Longing

Words unspoken things unsaid

Never remembering your presence

No words of encouragement

Wishing, hoping

Did you notice me?

Who am I?

Never nurtured by you

Never a hug or a kiss

Longing, wanting

A smile a sweet embrace

Your acceptance of me

Wanting you to be proud of me

Wanting you to just accept and notice me

A shadow in the dark you are

Longing for you

Praying for your love

Will you ever love me?

Daddy will you ever notice me

Longing for you

Unknown

The first time I met my biological Father was also the first time I remember meeting my older sister. I can still hear my mother's words as this big man I had never seen before walked through our door holding the hand of a little girl I had never seen before, but who resembled my mother. Dora made the introductions, her voice expressing a visible nervousness. I think this can be attributed to the fact she was just as surprised as the rest of us to see him. Prior to that moment I would hear stories as a child that my father never really acknowledged me as his daughter. I would then hear comments connecting me to him, like, *"Yes Ray is your Father."* They never said I looked like him, everyone always said I looked like my Aunt whom I had never met before. When I did finally meet my Aunt I could not understand what all the fuss was about. I did not think that I looked anything like her.

Dora said, *"Reese this is your older sister Nina and this man who is standing before you is your dad. His name is Ray."* I stood in the doorway stunned and somewhat in disbelief. We had never much discussed my father yet there had been whispers of his existence and comments describing who he was. However, I don't recall my mother discussing anything about me having a sister.

To be quite frank with you I did not care that much about meeting my father. Perhaps it was a result of his general disinterest in meeting me or being engaged in my life. Perhaps I had simply replaced him with other male figures in my life who were readily available and willing to love "little ole Reese." Whatever the case I was more interested in meeting my older sister. The first feeling I had when I met her was *"Wow!"* She was a welcome addition to the family albeit a previously well guarded secret. Prior to the knowledge of her there was my older brother, my younger brother, and sister, and of course me. Now instead of four peas in a pod we had five, how cool is that?

Trying to fully digest the reality of what had now become fact, I immediately began to study her physical features. Boy was she pretty, I thought. Nina had lighter skin than mine and it resembled my mothers' complexion. Now it actually made sense why I was darker than my mother I actually had my father's complexion. In term of physical features we shared very few noticeable ones. In my mind I started a mental checklist to compare her to my mother. Nina was dressed so fashionable in her chic jeans and flowered shirt, *check one*. When she smiled she displayed pretty dimples, like my mother, *check two*. Given the fact that she had the same skin color as mother, I had no choice but to give her *check three*. Yes, she was indeed my mothers' child and therefore by that admission my sibling.

At some point during that encounter my mother turned to me and asked, *"Reese what do you have to say to Ray?"* This was not only a probing question but in my opinion it was a cruel question. It was cruel in the sense that not only was I already feeling shy and awkward but now I was asked to essentially be the conversation initiator. How unfair was that, I was not the one that decided not to be involved in my child's life was I? This brings up an important lesson that parents who are in a *similar* situation can glean from this encounter. First, as parents of a child you need to be able to set aside your differences and try to create as amicable a situation as possible for your children.

If a parent is going to be introduced or reintroduced to a child then it should be done with the understanding that emotionally it will take some time for that child to adjust. One of the ways to ease this transition is to try to have that first casual meeting followed by a get together where the child can go to a park or something and hang out with the introduced parent. Of course such a get together should probably be done with the other parent within the same general vicinity. This is not to done to crowd the space of the "introduced parent" but more of an opportunity to allow the child to initially feel comfortable. The department of Children's services calls this a supervised visit.

Transitioning back to my initial encounter with Ray, my father, he followed my mother's question with a look that could have killed the dead. He said, *"Hey girl don't you hear your mother talking to you?"* Not the best first words of an introduction in my opinion. I felt so small and afraid under the glare of his stare. At that moment he seemed to tower over me at least by an extra couple of feet. I think his actual size was about six feet tall. Despite his lack of tact and kindness I did recognize his handsome features and deep booming voice. I also remember that he had the broadest shoulders that I had ever seen. I stood there in that moment thinking, *"I wonder if he could lift me onto his shoulders and carry me around?"* I know given the awkward nature of the moment that seems like a strange thought but that is actually the way a child's mind thinks. Remember it is the parents that are usually dealing with the emotions of a failed relationship and trying to vie for the child's affection. Never use children as a pawn because they are innocent in the whole ordeal and usually more willing to love unconditionally, despite the difficult nature of things.

Given Ray's charisma, smile and booming laugh I quickly concluded that he probably commanded attention. He was most likely especially popular with the ladies. Yep he was a candidate for the *TDH* club. Oh, you don't know about the *TDH* club. It is the **T**all **D**ark and **H**andsome Club and exclusively for those men who display such unique qualities. Some family members said his looks would actually cause women to melt in his presence. My mother described him as a womanizer and a fast talker. I must admit that even then as a little girl, I loved certain qualities about him. Particularly the way that he tilted his head and gave this teasingly contemptuous look when he was kidding with you. Although I had conflicting emotions about him I can definitely see why my mother fell for him.

It is so interesting that someone who can display such charismatic and attractive features can have such dark and almost sinister tendencies as well. He was always very loud when he spoke with my mother and me. It was as if when dealing with women we were more objects to be controlled and manipulated for his pleasure and purpose. Every encounter that I had with him after that point was no different. He was always loud and commanding in his speech and demeanor. I even think it could have been a psychological way of abusive power. Maybe he was saying to me, *"No matter what I am your daddy and don't you forget it little girl."* Yikes! It is strange that a man can believe that just because he fathered a child that he earned the right to receive that child's affection and respect. I privately wished that someone would remind him that he was the one that had been out of my life for the past seven years and not the other way around.

Somehow I summoned the courage to mumble the word, *"hi."* He rolled his eyes and titled his head back laughing vigorously. He then followed that up with a tactless and equally jarring question, *"Dora why is this little girl so timid?"* How could he expect me to say more when I previously did not even know that he existed? Why would he expect me to be more assertive? Did he want me to run to his outstretched arms and shower him with hugs and kisses' while exclaiming, *"Hello long lost daddy!"* "Come one let's be honest with one another, those are self-centered expectations", I thought. For his part he never picked me up. He did not even give me a hug or show any type of physical affection towards me. All he said in response to my *"hi"* was, *"hey girl."* Then we just stood there a few feet apart sort of sizing each other up and trying to figure what the other person was going to do. It made no never minds to me, I concluded, I was really more interested in getting to know my sister anyway.

After that initial meeting my father never really played an important part in my life. I can remember the first time that it really hit me how insignificant his role had been. The full awareness of it came many years later after I had been married and conceived my first two daughters.

I was in my hometown of Canton driving my oldest sister Nina to her boyfriend's house. On the way she said, *"Reese there goes our father."* Out of the five siblings at the time, Nina and I were the only ones who shared the same biological father and mother. As matter of fact my mother had given my sister up at birth to Ray's parents. This information comes from stories that had trickled down through the grapevine. It was actually Ray's parents that had initiated the arrangement; they asked if they could take care of my sister.

This was an attractive arrangement for my mother given her then present circumstances. She was barely a young woman, age 17, who already had a son to take care of. My mother and father had a tumultuous relationship anyway. So in the end my grandparents on Ray's side raised my sister. As far as I was concerned the living arrangement situation was what it was. I was simply glad to have an older sister. It took the some of the pressure associated with being the oldest daughter off of me. We were actually only a year apart but nonetheless she was still older. In all, the first four of Dora's children were stair stepper's being one year apart.

I didn't really care about seeing our father, but after spotting him, Nina insisted I stop and pull beside the car that Ray was sitting in. Nina then proceeded to get out and approach Ray's side of the car. The two of them have always shared a special bond because his parents raised her. Whenever I saw the two of them together the bond they shared was quite evident. It was probably the only identifiable emotion that I had as it relates to my father that feeling of resentment. I wish I had the same loving and close knit relationship that he had with Nina. The tenderness that he displayed with her was a side of him that I never personally received. In fact, he would hardly say a word to me when I was at my sister's house. *"How could he love one child more than the other,"* I wondered? These types of questions lingered in my mind whenever I saw the two of them together. I never said anything about this to anyone in my family, especially not my sister. This was due to the fact that I did not want her to feel as if I was jealous or that I was trying to take her place in our father's heart. All I really wanted was the same connection that she had. Since this would not become a reality I chose to bottle up those emotions, in a private space within my heart.

These secret emotions that I had bottled up in my heart provide another opportunity to enlighten parents about children's perspective in this situation. Pay special attention to the Tip that comes at the end of this chapter. Understand that if a child is going through a difficult time in their life it is you as the parent that must seek to engage that child in a way that they feel comfortable sharing these feelings. I don't believe that Dora was adequately or effectively able to assess my emotional challenges. Coming from a place of dysfunction herself, she was not equipped to deal with what it meant to be a nurturer. This is not to excuse her because if she truly wanted to be a nurturer, there are resources that exist and existed then, that could have aided her in resolving some of her own internal conflict.

For whatever reason she chose not to research or pursue those resources and as a result we both suffered unnecessarily. Your willingness as a parent to deal with your own past dysfunction will often determine the level of dysfunction of future generations. If there are no answers provided for children about issues pertaining to their life, or what they know about yours then many times they will draw their own conclusions.

After our initial meeting together, I remember Nina always wanting me to come over to her house. We spent time on the weekends together, both of us trying to make up for lost time. I was actually relieved and excited that she took me under her wings. We eventually became inseparable and very close. I loved being with her and spending as much time as we could together although I was not as comfortable with the rest of that side of the family. Particularly my paternal grandparents, as I often wondered how they felt about me. For their part, my grandparents did not mistreat me in anyway, but they did often display an emotional distance. Sometimes I felt that they only dealt with me because Nina desired to have me around. So in other words rather than seeing me as an equally valuable grandchild, in my opinion they simply accommodated me. Even as I struggled with these feelings of isolation, and invisibility in their eyes I remained silent. I did not want them to think I was ungrateful or that I secretly desired them to love me unconditionally like my sister. I never asked to be born, just like she didn't, where was the justice?

As Nina approached Ray's side of the car I heard her say, *"Reese is in the car."* In response he did not even bother to look my way or attempt to acknowledge me. No *"how ya doing sweetheart"*, or even a smile? This of course while painful was no surprise to me. Given the fact I had not seen him in almost ten years I did not expect that he would have much to say. While we had both given up hope of a Father-daughter connection Nina apparently had not. *"Ray, Reese and her kids are in the car...you need to meet your granddaughters,"* she insisted. Only then did he finally look up from what he was doing. Laurel was about four years old and Amber was barely two. I had dressed them both in matching legging outfits that day. Although they were dressed the same, they had different colors. I often did that because it made the both of them look fashionably cute, but each had their own unique looks at the same time. Laurel's outfit was light blue and Amber's was pink. Nina then opened the car door and said *"girls get out I want you to meet your grandfather."* My oldest daughter Laurel was confused because she had no idea that she had a grandfather that was living. Up to this point I had never talked about Ray to my girls, for obvious reasons.

Laurel being the outspoken child that she is blurted out, *"That's not our grandfather, and mommy does not have a daddy."* I was thinking to myself, *"this should have been a proud moment for both my girls and me but instead it was again another awkward moment with Ray."* They were meeting him for the first time and this meeting was surrounded by the same confusion and bitterness that had defined my first meeting with Ray. Again instead of seeking redemption and displaying reconciliatory behaviors Ray again acted disinterested in either me or my daughters.

When he got out of the car he did not even try to pick up either of the girls or try to shake their hands. Nina tried to get him to hold Amber but it was not happening. She went from crying to screaming and held out her arms frantically for me. Ray had this perplexed look on his face as if he was incapable of assessing or changing the situation. Nina was not happy about the results of her efforts, she apparently had hoped for more. I on the other hand was resigned to sit in the car and observe from a safe distance. Even still, I felt a sick feeling deep inside as my heart dropped into the pit of my stomach. At that moment it was as if I was peering and seeing life through the eyes of my daughters. I momentarily reverted back to life as a little girl with a wounded spirit, once again craving the love of a father.

Even prior to meeting their grandfather that day Laurel was reluctant to step out of the car. Nina had to lead her by the hand, and she even picked up Amber who had started to cry. Maybe even though I had never communicated the difficulty surrounding the awkwardness of my relationship with Ray they sensed something was not right. Children have the ability not only to sense the energy surrounding a situation, but also to read individuals' feelings towards them. As I continued to observe the scene being played out from the car, I began to fume. I harshly chided myself for expecting him to show love and affection for my girls. *"Reese, girl you know better, how could he display with them what he could not even give you?"* I thought.

Unfortunately we would be confined to solely relating to each other as two strangers connected only by blood, and nothing more. As a child when you hear the word *daddy, father, or papa* you immediately associate those terms with *love, tenderness, protection, and warrior.* For me these associations were not there I always recognized a void in my spirit and a lack of identifying or connecting with these terms. At last I opened my mouth to speak but the words never came out. *"Was I still a little girl being manhandled by a six foot man?"* Defiantly I thought enough is enough, *"Nina, bring my girls back to the car, because I'm ready to go."* This was said with an air of indifference but the tone of my voice was one of finality concerning the situation. There was a resolute and expressed firmness from someone who was tired of believing in change only to be let down time after time. My father further justified the wisdom in my resolve by not even speaking a word of protest.

Even though this happened some time ago I remember this incident like it was yesterday. The drive back to Columbus was long and exhausting and still smarting from the incident my emotions ranged from anger and sadness to eventual numbness. I think that the numbness was more a feeling that I was accustomed to. Growing up I became accustomed to my Father's calloused attitude and perhaps had adopted a variation of his attitude myself. However seeing what affect it had on my children caused me to wish Nina and I had not run into my father. I did not want them to experience that raw, blemished aspect of my life.

When commercials featuring fathers and daughters came on they often made me cry. One commercial in particular sticks out in my mind. It depicts a daughter growing up while the song *You are my Hero* play's in the background. The daughter is shown on her wedding day with her father looking at her with loving eyes. His expression read's, *"I can't believe that daddy's little girl is all grown up."* He is about to let her go. The commercial then shows the two of them dancing. The final scene is of him writing the check for the wedding with tears in his eyes. There is also a brief flashback of his daughter dancing on her father's feet as a little girl. I always envisioned sharing this type of memory with my father. *"And who would give me away at my wedding anyway,"* I wondered? Some may simply see the commercial as a shameless marketing plug for a product. For me it signified the lost opportunities and never to be experienced memories. Thankfully, my saving grace was the fact that my daughters would never dance alone on their wedding date, their father would be right there with them.

In addition to that commercial, watching a movie that depicted a father or grandfather playing a significant role in a child's life would wound my heart. Again trying to be strong and in control I would chide myself. *"Why are you getting so emotional about this Reese?"* I mean it's not my fault that my father chose not to have a relationship with me. It's also not my fault that he never reached out to get to know his grandchildren or have a relationship with them. There is nothing that I could have done, and nothing that I can do now. As matter of fact although it is a sad situation it is really his loss, and not ours. Look at who I have become, a productive and healthy wife, mother, and citizen of the global society. Not only that but the loss felt by his absence I now channel as energy towards building relationships with my husband and my four children. Even still, I could not get rid of the empty feelings and disappointment that I felt. Truly the love of a father is something that is deeper than words or thoughts can define and fully understand.

Why is a father's love so vital in a young girl's life? As stated earlier, it molds who she is as a person. It also helps to define how she views young boys and men. A Father's love teaches her not to be afraid to open up and express herself with the opposite sex. As matter of fact even women who become promiscuous early, many times are simply craving that affection and attention from a man. The way in which they seek and ultimately find that might be distasteful and shameful to some conservative onlookers, but it is important not to judge. Do your best not to be overly critical of someone's story, especially if you don't know their History.

TIP 6: *Ask them how their day went*: It makes them feel like you really care about what's going on in their lives. It also teaches children social skills and the process of interacting with people. When you think about some of the awkwardness that I dealt with in this chapter you can better understand the importance of healthy and positive interaction. Remember the development of a child's engagement with the world will come from how they communicate with you. It also allows them to better process their feelings. Finally it allows you as the parent to have the opportunity to understand how your child thinks and feels. How else will they know that they can come to you when they are going through something at school or just dealing with a difficult issue or have questions? If you don't start that practice when they are young then chances are it will become increasingly more difficult when they become older. A good time to do this is at the dinner table, which is why even if a percentage of the week is microwave eat and run meals, make sure that you try to eat together as a family as much as possible.

Chapter 7: My First Visit and the Other Sister

<u>*Just like me*</u>

When I giggle and laugh

And make a big scene

Like a mirror reflecting

You laugh just like me

Your skin may be lighter

Your hair might be long

My bangs might stick out

Your teeth overgrown

But at the end of the day

When it's all said and done

A mirror speaks volumes

You are just like me

Rudo

My first visit to Nina's house was approximately one week after we had first met. I believe it was my Aunt on my father's side who picked me up. When my Aunt came to pick me up Nina rode with her so that we could chat on the way. As we got close to her house she pointed out the school she attended. I noted the fact that it was right down the street from her house. I wondered if she walked to school or if they take her to school? *"Of course they took her,"* I concluded, *"what a stupid question."* There were so many beautiful and spacious houses lining the streets, I could only whisper, *"Wow."* It is amazing to think that there are actually people living in these houses. I began to visualize the backyards behind these beautiful houses. There must have been nice manicured yards and plenty of trees for shade.

This of course was quite different from the projects where I was raised. Nina's house was comfortably nestled at the end of the street, it was gray. As we parked and I approached the front door I could see it had a huge porch. You had to go through a second door before you actually entered the house. Of course this was back during the seventies which was a period in which houses were built differently. I can trace the specific time period by the fact that my father fashionably wore one of those pull over dashiki's that men and women wore. My father's was multi-colored and he sported an afro hairdo.

I'll never forget Mrs. Peters, my grandmother whom I was meeting for the first time. I remember her saying, *"Come in child."*, as I hesitated at the door. I was frozen halfway between the door and the porch as I fought with feelings of dread and apprehension. Mrs. Peters can be best described as a tiny lady who always kept her hair done nicely. She reminded me of one of those mothers' on the television show, *Leave it to Beaver*. She always had on an apron and kept the house immaculate. I wondered if that was the way that Ray visualized what a woman's role was supposed to be in the home. Mrs. Peters believed in taking care of her family and making sure that dinner was served in a timely manner. I could tell that she loved my sister Nina as though she was a child from her own womb. Three of her grown children lived in the house along with my sister. Those three children included my father (*when he was around*), my Aunt, and my Uncle Robby.

Nina of course was spoiled rotten by her grandma. She guided me through the house and into the bedroom that she shared with my Aunt. The first thing that I noticed is that there were two beds in the room. I remember the fact that my sister's bed was closest to the door. My Uncle Robby slept down the hall with my Father, I could only assume. I never called Mr. and Mrs. Peters Grandma or Grandpa. To their credit they never suggested or asked me to. Mrs. Peters loved to pile lots of covers on the bed, which I liked. During the wintertime it was always warm and toasty. I believed that if we were butter Nina and I would have melted under the heat of those covers, like margarine on hot toast! *"Mmmm..."* I loved spending time with my sister. Just being around her made me truly happy.

The thing that struck me the most about the house was the bathroom. I could not believe how big their bathroom was compared to mine in the projects. Again, for you fellas' reading this book I know this is probably more of a woman's pleasure. Still, I do know of men who can also appreciate a well kept bathroom. For the rest of you, men and women who may not be able to relate humor me and pay attention to the exercise below.

To visualize what I saw close your eyes for a moment. Now imagine yourself walking into a five star hotel like the Hilton, or Ritz Carlton. To really raise the stakes let's say you probably paid $150-$200 per night for a single room. When you first walk into your room where's one of the first places you would look? The bathroom probably if you are like most people. Isn't it grand? Towel's appeared as though they cost about $50-$80 per towel right? The bathroom looks like it has never been used. And if it doesn't then uh…you might want to call room service. Sometimes they even wrap a bow around the toilet so that you have to tear it off before you can use it. Sound familiar? Good, then this gives you a sense of the way I felt walking into the Peter's bathroom.

Mrs. Peter's bathroom was so colossal that if she wanted to she could convert it to an extra bedroom. There was lots of cabinet space that served as storage for towels. Also there was a large bathtub, like a swimming pool and a sizeable sink. Thinking back to how modernized the layout was I have concluded that their design, and bathroom were conceived of and created, well before their time. My sister, by having the ability to live in such an exquisite dwelling, seemed to enjoy a luxury uncommon to most adolescence, including me. When I would visit them I loved taking baths in that colossal bathtub. This was primarily made possible due to the fact that Mrs. Peter's believed that as the saying goes, *"Cleanliness was next to Godliness."* After we played outside and got all grungy and dirty we were promptly placed into the bath. Nina and I did not resist at all and would actually respond with squeals of delight. We would pretend that we were on big ships or in a huge swimming pool.

Other memories that we shared included hanging out with her friends in the neighborhood. There was actually a small park in the back of her house that we would walk to. At the park there were live animals it was almost like a small zoo. I remember peering through the fence for instance and attempting to feed the animals. Let's say a zebra came near the fence, I might offer him food, if I had some.

Mr. Peter's, my grandfather, was a short round little man. I remember Mrs. Peters called him *"Will"* and they both seemed to love one another, the children, and grandchildren. While she kept the house immaculate and embraced the role of nurturer, he was bread winner, busy working outside of the home. His demeanor was very quiet and serene mostly, but sometime he could be spotted cracking jokes. In particular he loved poking fun at us grandchildren. Nina actually took to calling him *"daddy"* which is a very common practice for children who have a male figure in their life that become surrogate parents. Something internal within a child recognizes that there is supposed to be both a mother and a father in a family. This is reinforced by social observance, and messages communicated in the media.

It is funny how Mr. Peters would pronounce my name *"Re-e-se"* because he put special emphasis on each syllable. This was the case particularly if he was razzing me or wanting to get my attention. He would always ask the same question when I came over. He would start off with, *"Gal do you talk at all?"* It was of course a rhetorical question because obviously he knew that I did, but probably felt like I spoke very little. As I mentioned I was extremely shy around both he and Mrs. Peters, even though they were more sociable than my father, Ray. How could Ray have fallen so far from the tree I wondered? Mr. Peters wore overalls on every other occasion except on Sunday's when he would get dressed up for church. He reminded me of a farmer both in mannerism as well as overall appearance.

He thoroughly enjoyed working in his garden out in the backyard. When I came over in the summers he would show me the process of how plants grew. This was fascinating to observe the life cycle of an assortment of vegetation.   Although the relationship I had with the Peter's did not feel like a granddaughter-grandparent relationship they were always cordial. To the best of their ability they tried to make sure I felt welcome. I wondered if, even though they never verbalized it, they were responding out of love for me. The only other possibility was that they wanted to make sure that Nina had a playmate and sensed I was important to her.

Another vivid memory that made me feel even more de-valued by my father and isolated from that side of the family was meeting my, *other sister*. One weekend in particular turned out to be both unusual and very heartbreaking for me. Of course by this time visiting my sister had become ritual and I anticipated going to her house to visit. On this particular weekend however my sister and I were first introduced to another girl. I don't even remember the details of how the other little girl came into the picture; but years later I heard my mother talking to some of her friends about my father and his family. She was saying that when they found out she was five months pregnant with his second child, they treated her very distant and cold. The day she attempted to tell Mrs. Peters she was pregnant again, she was not allowed in the house.

As insensitive as it may have seemed, part of the logic Mrs. Peters was probably using was based on what was going on in the house at the time. Apparently my father was in the house with his new girlfriend who was also pregnant at the time. Clearly my father, the womanizer, did not waste any time replacing the women in his life. I can only imagine what that scene would have been like had my mother, Dora, been allowed in the house to confront my father. Dora was impacted by the fact that his family never really accepted me as being his child. In their mind it was inconceivable that their precious son could impregnate a woman that he had already fathered a child with and they were now raising, even given his history with women. Go figure the logic in that right? Needless to say, Mrs. Peters slammed the door in my mother's face and told her, *"Don't you ever come to this house again."*

I guess they certainly were in no mood to raise another child. In fact I later came to find out that my father's parents never really liked my mother at all. This of course was information that a child was not supposed to be privy to but through that trusty old grapevine, news often trickled down to me. I also felt like this was probably due to the fact that they did not feel like Dora was worthy to receive affection from their son, who came from a Christian home of all things. I heard that explanation on a couple of occasions. I used to think, "If *this man is my father like my mother says, why am I not brown skinned like my sister?"* After all he was supposed to be the father of both of us right? On one occasion I heard that when I was born my father actually came to the hospital to see my mother. He probably came for selfish reasons, like to make sure he was not the father. When he first looked at me apparently he said, *"Now I know she is not mine. She is way too dark to be mine."* I could never understand how any man could say something so hurtful to a woman and in the presence of an innocent newborn baby. My mother of course reacted how any self respecting woman would have acted. She ordered him to leave the hospital. I thought, no wonder he didn't want me as a child, I didn't look like my sister. My skin was not light brown like hers when she was born. It is also worth noting that over the years through that same grapevine I would hear whispers of yet another sister out there. Call it irony or fate, but in terms of this other sister's features I heard she looked like me, and that her skin was as dark as mine.

Now that I have given you a little additional history concerning my unwanted and uncelebrated birth, let me talk more about the *"other sister."* As mentioned earlier during a weekend visit with my sister the bombshell was dropped. Nina and I were sitting on the porch playing. When our grandparents told my sister that a little girl was coming over to meet her. I don't recall much excitement from Nina and of course I was not that excited either. I think the purpose of them explaining this to Nina was so that she would be prepared when the time arrived. She was used to getting her own way, being the center of attention and this was obviously not good news. I think that one of the reasons that Nina openly accepted me is that we had the same mother and father. Meeting a little girl who was conceived while Ray was with another woman would be hard. This would especially hard when combined with the fact that Nina was just finding out about this additional bit of news. Of course by the same token it was especially difficult for me since I was still trying to position myself to be accepted and loved equally by Ray's parents. I also desperately wanted to horde my sister, Nina's affection. Now, I feared there would be even more competition.

Finally, the girl arrived, and the first thing that became evident is that she was light-brown skinned just like my sister. Talk about feeling like the *"odd girl out."* The interesting thing is that Ray's parents were so accepting of this girl. I thought back to the lukewarm reception that I received. I thought, *"Why are they so accepting of her? How do they know she really is our father's daughter? We're all around the same age hmm, how is this possible?*   In addition, there was a nagging feeling that I got deep down in my gut. I felt like I had met this girl somewhere before although I could not remember where at first. Then all of a sudden it hit me like a bully on a school campus, she had attended the same school that I did. When I had that realization I could not believe it. I stood there in absolute shock. Not only was that strange to have been going to school with your own sister and not even know it but, I wondered what made her so special.

Then I thought about that moment in the hospital when Ray said, *"she can't be my daughter she is too dark skinned,"* in reference to me. I finally understood why she had received unequivocal acceptance. It was the fact that she had light-brown skin like my sister made whatever inconveniences or awkwardness of her existence a mere formality to be dealt with. Not only that as my thoughts swirled I wondered why they did not refer to us as sisters'. I knew I would never feel the same way about her when I saw her at school, knowing what I now know.

Of course I was too afraid to seek answers to these questions. When we played together that day I silently prayed that my sister, Nina, would not like her more than she liked me. Playtime should always be a time where a child can engage with fantasy or just relax. During this particular playtime it was not very relaxing the three of us hanging out for the first time. In retrospect I think of the broader implications of this whole scenario. While each girl inevitably struggled with her own emotions and perspective of the situation I can only express my internal process. I wondered how a father could reject something he helped to create? To me a child is the greatest gift that one can receive.

That day as I sat there playing with sisters who each had skin as contrasting as our individual pasts, I made a vow that if I had children they would have two parents. Not only that we would both give them unconditional love. I on the other hand did not live in that reality and so all I could do was try to push everything out of my mind. Whatever my father did or did not do was in the past and I could not become consumed with it. My favorite line to rebuff those negative thoughts was, *"who needs a father anyway?"* I was determined that if he chose to deny me then I would just do the same. There is an old African saying, *"If love is rough with you then you must be rough with love."*

TIP 7: *Spend one-on-one time together with your child*: Set aside time for you and your child to do something special together. Children love one-on-one time with Dad and or Mom. It makes them feel special like a King or Queen for the day. As a matter of fact you can even make up a holiday. How about a "Good report card day"? They will cherish this one-on-one time together always, it will be embedded in their subconscious. (Here are more examples of one-on-one activities)

- *Father/Daughter & Mother/Son Date Night*: Dad takes her to dinner, and shows her how a man is supposed to pull out their chair and open doors for them. Talk to her about how to chew, and what the difference is between a salad fork and a regular fork. Mother's do the same thing for your son. Also talk to them in a very sociable way so that years later they will know how to carry on an intelligent conversation with future dates.

- *Father/Child recreation time*: This is a time where Fathers can play activities such as catch with either your son or daughter. You can also take your children camping or fishing. And yes even those activities that appear to be something more suited to a boy or vice versa, are really suitable for either gender.

- *Father/Child "You choose activity"*: Just like it sounds this is where you allow the child to pick an activity instead of having an organized activity for them. You will be surprised and amazed at what they come up with.

- *Father/Child treats night*: This is where you take the child out for a tasty treat like an ice cream. Baskin Robbins is one of the more popular ice cream spots and provides flavor filled treats for any sweet lover. Depending on your demographic there will most likely be a popular venue that serves treats.

Chapter 8: My Uncle Robby

Little niece

All the colors of summer

All the figs of spring

Connected to one another

Part of the same family tree

I accepted your imperfections

And cherished your acceptance of me

For I was no distant stranger

I was your "favorite niece"

I loved how you spoiled me

Called me out from the crowd

You were not ashamed to speak truth

Your support of me renowned

And when the news came

That you would no longer be around

I stood somber in my stupor

I felt so lost in the crowd

Rudo

---

*B*ased on the last chapter it probably will come as no surprise to you that I never truly connected with my father's side of the family. However, I will add a disclaimer, because there was one person that I did connect with on my father's side. It was my father's brother, my Uncle Robby. He was a little shorter than my father and his body was lankier, in my opinion. To me he more resembled his Father, Mr. Peters. He did not have the handsome looks that my father possessed, but he had a very big heart. From the first time I met him he treated me like I was family and made me feel a sense of unconditional love. Anytime he would meet me he would greet me with a great big bear hug. He referred to me as his *"little niece"*. Not only that but he did not shun me in public. Upon spotting me around town, he always complimented me and was accustomed to referring to me as his *"Favorite niece"*.

I always looked forward to spending time with my Uncle Robby. Years ago mysteriously my Uncle Robby was brutally and senselessly murdered. I think it must be somewhere stored in the catalog of America's Unsolved Mysteries. Given the significance that he had in my life I'll never forget that fateful call I received from my sister Nina. It was that much more difficult for me because I was not prepared to accept the loss of someone so special. Also, I could not understand how someone so caring could be killed by someone so insensitive. It seemed to be too broad a contrast for my child-like mind. Many people criticized him for being an alcoholic but I never had any hang ups with that. I mean, if he could accept me for who I was then I certainly would accept him for any flaws that he might have had. As matter of fact when he died I believe that a small piece of my heart was destroyed with him. As a child I sometimes secretly wished that he was my father, instead of Ray.

I thought of all the wonderful memories that I would no longer enjoy. Those memories read like a eulogy, similar to the ones read at gravesides of loved ones. I knew I would miss the acknowledgement that I receive from him when I went to visit my sister. I would also miss the smiles and hugs that he gave me. When he died there was a sense of finality with regards to another matter as well. I knew that any hopes that I previously held for truly becoming part of the family were now buried at least six feet underground forever. Although not wanting to let on how special he was to me, I did grieve silently.

Unfortunately I did not attend his funeral, but in my own child-like way not going was a survival technique. I wanted to remember the fun-loving Uncle I had come to know. The bond that we shared grew beyond mere blood ties, and reciprocal acts of kindness. We were a band of battle tested warriors in the fight to embrace self. Rejected by many we provided each other with a sense of self-worth and unconditional love. The rest of the family never knew I felt this strongly towards Uncle Robby because I never explained it to them.

They would not have understood why anyway. They were too busing ignoring or distancing themselves from us, him for his alcoholism and me for my unwanted existence and unpopular skin color.

I remember one day I was walking past one of my Uncle Robby's favorite hangouts following his murder. Even though it is irrational I recall just standing there waiting for him to come out and greet me like he always did. I visualized him coming towards me with this big smile on his face. He might lean over and say to his friends, *"Hey guy's, here's my niece, my brother's daughter."* He was the only one who ever truly verbalized that I was family. He was the only one that genuinely felt proud to have me as part of the family. Probably somewhat selfishly I wish that he had lived longer so my children could have met him. I know he would have made a wonderful Uncle to my children. He undoubtedly would have loved them with the same unconditional love as he displayed towards me. I was also saddened by the fact that he never had the opportunity to have children of his own. I know he would have made a great father. His life was senselessly taken away before he had the opportunity to live life to the fullest. Even though he never experienced Fatherhood, somehow I hope that our bond gave him a basic sense of what it would have been like.

Later in life, my sister came to live with us for a while. The first thing that my mother did was set some hard fast ground rules. One rule was that my father was not allowed to pick her up or take her out without first making arrangements with my mother. This obviously created some tension between them. To compound the matter, there was already the existence of tension due to the fact that my father and mother had a very tumultuous relationship as teenagers. My father probably felt that my mother was being vindictive by taking Nina back from his parents. The tension between the two families was atrocious.

This tension came to a head one day when my father came to pick my sister up after she had moved in with us. My mother was at a girlfriend Ilene's house and we had just let Ray and Uncle Robby into the house. I remember Nina running and jumping into his arms. I proceeded to stand there and watch this loving interaction between the two of them take place. He threw her up in the air affectionately calling her by his favorite nickname for her, his *"Little peaches."* During this entire ordeal he never said a word at all to me. I should have been used to being belittled or made to feel invisible by him. My Uncle Robby did however not only speak to me but he gave me the biggest hug of my life. It was a sort of moment of vindication for my father's rudeness. Ray continued by asking, *"Nina are you glad to see Daddy?"* Nina exclaimed, "Yes Daddy!" Meanwhile I stood there and silently cried my heart out. *"Daddy…"* I wished that I could hear what it sounded like calling him that coming from my mouth. I wish I could see him smile as broadly for me as he did for Nina. *"Daddy…"* I wish I could feel his arms around me, throwing ME up in the air and tickling ME. *"Daddy!"*

Ray then asked Nina if she was ready to go. Now I knew he was not allowed to take her unless my mother was present. So in the sternest voice I could muster I said, *"You are not allowed to take her unless Dora is here."* I was standing there trying to appear intimidating with my feet squared and my little hands on my hips. I was trying to make my voice as mean sounding as possible because I was trying to hurt him. Inside I was fuming. Anger and jealousy swirled like a volcano that had been dormant for years but had reared its ugly head. I was furious because he had not acknowledged me once since he stepped in our house. My Uncle Robby was standing next to my father during this exchange holding my sister.

My father suddenly turned towards me and spat out very harshly, **"SHUT UP YOU LITTLE BLACK BASTARD!!"** Even today I can still feel the sting of those degrading words pass through my ears. Since I knew what a bastard child was I stood there frozen in disbelief. As children we were always referred to as bastard children since our fathers were not around. Now in yet another strange twist of fate, I was standing front and center in front of the enemy. I was being called a bastard by the very person who had abandoned me. The one for whom the term was made popular. When he said this to me it felt just like he had taken his mammoth of a hand and slapped me as hard as he could across my face. Those words still cut through my heart like a knife and bring tears to my eyes whenever I hear a child being referred to as a *"bastard child."*

My Uncle Robby immediately asked my father why he would say such a thing to me. I could barely see through the tears that had started to well up in my eyes. I screamed, "I AM GOING TO GET MY MOTHER!" I knew she was at her friend Ilene's at that time. I ran as fast as my little legs could carry me to Ilene's house. When I finally got there, I just blurted out to my mother what had happened and what my father had said to me. My mother Dora could hardly make out what I was saying because I was crying so hard and speaking so fast. Those words, "LITTLE BLACK BASTARD," were etched in my heart for a very long time. I could overlook the fact that he never really wanted me, but when he called me a *"little black bastard,"* as a child I truly felt lost. I still lose it and get emotional when I recall that moment. I hate to hear a child being referred to as a bastard!

I remember my mother running to the house and me doing my best to keep up with her. She as hot as a tea kettle and I honestly think she could have killed my father with her bare hands that day. I think her raging emotions came in part from the pain of being rejected by my father and his family as well. It was the last straw in a wounding bond of rejection and a saga of emotional abuse that we both were victims of. When we arrived at the house, which seemed like an eternity later, my father and mother argued bitterly. I remember my Uncle Robby restraining my mother. She told my father it was wrong of him to say what he had said to me. None of us could believe or even anticipate the words that came out of his mouth next. He broke out in laughter and said, *"Oh please I was only playing with her!"* My mother looked at him in disbelief and screamed, *"I can't believe you!*

You don't play with a child like that! What is the matter with you? You are so sick!"

After they left with my sister I remember sitting on the front porch steps. The only thought that remained in my mind was, *"I hate this man. He's not worthy to be anyone's father. He's a bum."* Years have passed and I think about the old saying, *"Time heals all wounds."* I don't know if the saying always hold true. To me there is nothing more powerful than a Father's Love, especially the love between a father and his daughter. The love, admiration and respect should be mutual, powerful, and everlasting. A daughter should know that her father is there to catch her when she falls, to help her through her first broken heart. A father should also be there to give her away on that special day, her wedding day. If time does heal all wounds then time must have been postponed in my case.

I feel that the individual(s) who murdered my Uncle Robby did me a grave injustice. They robbed me of a relationship with a man who loved me from the moment I was born and never denied or rejected me. I have always thought how different my life would have been had he still been alive.

TIP 8: *Don't try to buy your child's love*: Children know the difference between genuine love and "store bought" love. It's okay to shower your children with the best material things that life has to offer (clothes, toys, car, and houses) but that is not what they need the most. Your unconditional love and attention mean more and will last longer. It reminds me of a billboard I saw one time that says, _your child wants your presence more than your presents_.

Chapter 9: Father's Day-the Dreaded Holiday

**Daddy's Little Girl**

What is about those words so endearing?

What is it that causes a longing to hear?

Why is that I always wanted a mention

Of Daddy's Little girl to be said in a sentence

Truthfully I wonder if you even cared

I wasn't given your name

No inheritance shared

I was closer to Nina on the weekend visits

The house was so lavish the scenery exquisite

Affection and attention that I longed to receive

From you never came, I continued to believe

I desired so much to be your baby girl

For you to love and protect me

And shower me with the world

To whisper in my ear, as I twirled my curl

"I love you my princess you're "Daddy's Little Girl"

Dad the first time my husband uttered these words

My hearts dam was broken

And spewed forth new emotion

Tears of pain is what it hurled

That was mixed with feelings of deep resentment

Now that I've found strength to overcome

Daddy's Little Girl, seeks contentment

Rudo

One of the most difficult Holiday's of the year that I encountered as a child was Father's Day. Until I actually had children of my own this holiday only represented rejection and the pain of what I did not have. I remember being forced as a child to make things in school for my father that would only end up in the trash since I had no one to give them to. I never put much effort into my father's day gifts or cards anyway. Part of the reason was due to the fact I never quite knew what to say inside the card. It's hard saying *Daddy I Love You,* to someone who wasn't around. It was hard especially given the fact you were not accustomed to receiving those words yourself.

I never understood why I had to partake in making a Father's day gift and card in school when my father was absent both from my life and my home. I would have preferred, as a child, not to have this dreaded holiday pushed on me. It would have been better if I would have at least had the opportunity to determine who I would have liked to make my gift for. I would have made a gift for my grandmother instead of my father, since she was the one that was there for me. Perhaps as a society that is what we need to implement. A National Holiday that celebrates unconventional families, and surrogate parents. That way all children feel valued.

As I got older, I would speak up and tell my teachers that there was no Father in our home. For the most part this day was not a joyful time for me, but somehow the teachers never seemed to catch on to this fact. They could never understand why it took me so long to get started on my card or little gifts that we were supposed to make. Whenever a teacher would come by to check my progress on the assignment they would usually discover that my canvass was blank. Trying to make a card or complete a gift for my Father was very painstaking because it required me to tap into an emotional space that was based on the relationship we shared. When it came to tapping into that space there was no love or affection just sadness and emptiness. I was empty and lacking such resources as emotional security from the father department. As a result, I did not care what my classmates or teachers thought about how aesthetic or heartwarming my Father's Day creations where. This is probably why my cards and gifts were usually the ugliest. As matter of fact I don't think any of my cards said **Happy Father's Day!** They usually just said *"Happy Day"* or *"To Father."*

I was extremely relieved when I finished elementary school because I would no longer have to participate in making those stupid cards or gifts to give a father that did not exist. Teachers always gave me sympathetic looks as if to say, *"Oh my God you poor thing, no father in the home."* I loathed this look of pity because I did not want people's pity. I even used to tell my friends that I did not need a Father to make me feel special. I then explained that, *"I did not want to make a stupid gift for someone who did not give a damn about me anyway."* I also made excuses such as, *"Fathers are mean and all they do is tell you what to do."* This was a shield of course a façade that I put up to hide the fact that I was jealous of kids with fathers. I hated thinking about the fact that some fortunate kids did have fathers that loved them. I would tell my friends that my grandmother who was raising me was both my father and mother, and she was all that I needed.

As I got older as Father's Day approached I summoned the courage to stretch myself. I would sometimes go to the stores and read heartwarming Father's Day Cards. I wondered what it would have actually felt like as a child to have purchased a card and actually wrote *"I love you Daddy,"* on the inside. And not just write it but actually feel it and mean it sincerely. Some of the cards made me smile, but most cards just brought tears to my eyes. I wished that I could have purchased a card and presented it to my father and that he would have been happy to receive it. I remember that after I met my

Uncle Ernest I would sometimes send him cards and it would make him feel good. I think that Uncle Ernest was probably the closest thing that I had to a father.

Having my own children helped to fill some of the void because it was important that they celebrated the joys of having their father in their lives. I always make sure that Father's Day for my husband is always a special day. The kids buy cards that reflect the love that they have for their father. Then they take their school made gifts, in addition to gifts that we buy together as a family and we place it on a special table for their Dad. When he first comes down the stairs in the morning, cards and gifts are the first things that he sees'. As a mother I can tell they put so much love and care in making their gifts because they are always so excited to see their Daddy's face. This feeling of anticipation and joy that a child feels is what I had hoped to experience as a child. Now I live somewhat vicariously through the experiences of my children, which is somewhat therapeutic.

Each one of our children will tell their Father *"Happy Father's Day!"* I also make sure I get him a card to let him know not only how much our children appreciate him as a father, but my appreciation for him as well. I let him know that I specifically am thankful that he makes a home for me and his children. He is the King of our home and he knows this. He makes a big deal out of displaying his cards and gifts with pride. Father's Day celebrations now reflect not the pain and alienation of the past but represent a future that is full of hope, joy, and possibility. Hugs, Kisses, Smiles, and Appreciation, these are the words that one should associate with Father's Day.

My sister would on occasion call me and update me about my Father's status and activities. She did this despite the fact that I never asked about him at all. With maturity and age the importance of this information became less of a focus, more diminished in my eyes. I guess Nina just felt like it was her duty to share although it usually only served to upset her or agitate me. Once she called to inform me that our Father was getting married. I guess she wanted me to, despite our rocky past to feel some type of joy in his celebration. I remember responding very defensively, *"He's not my Father, he's your father. Further, I could care less about him getting married! Hopefully he'll treat his wife well because he never gave our mother or me a second thought."* When she called me and told me about the birth of his son I was really angry because I thought, *"How can this man keep fathering children and not taking care of them?"* My heart bled for this child because my father had never been a father to any of his children except my sister. What kind of father would he be to his newborn son? He finally got the son he so desperately wanted, now what?

It always seemed my sister wanted me to love my Father as she did, even though he was never there for me. He never once showed an ounce of affection for me. Whenever we spoke about him I would usually make some snide cold response about him. I could tell that it hurt her feelings, but I did not care. I was jealous of the relationship that she shared with him, a relationship that I longed to have. She would always say I never made an effort to get to know him. In my defense I thought, *"Why is it up to me to get to know him? He is my Father! He denied me from the very moment I was born. The only reason that he even looks or says anything to me is because of you…I wanted to love him from the moment I was conceived. Why then did he not love me?"*

Nina of course could not understand the agony that I felt. She could not relate to my longing for acceptance by Ray and his family. She never heard the whispers or the remarks said behind closed doors and I never told her. She was therefore an innocent bystander in the dark. She was the child that received love, by the evil parent. I on the other hand was Cinderella looking for a glass slipper so that things would change for me. Maybe I suppressed my emotions and did not divulge anything to her because I was afraid it might leak out to them. If that happened they might not have allowed me to keep seeing her fearing that I would turn her against my father or them. So I just chose to put on a brave and happy face when I was at her house pretending like everything was ok.

Privately I think I believed that if I stayed around their house long enough, maybe Ray would have a change of heart. Perhaps he would begin to notice that I actually existed. Maybe out of the corner of his eye he might acknowledge, *"Damn she does look like me. I guess I have not one but two beautiful princesses."* Maybe he might grow to love me as he loved Nina.

I remember Nina calling me one day to tell me our Father was in the hospital and that he was really sick. I don't know why, but on this particular day I just blew up at her. I remember saying, *"Why do you feel like you have to call me and tell me about this man? I don't know him. He has never given me a second thought. All these years, not once has he tried to find out how I am doing….What I am doing. Or even to check if I am dead or alive!"* We begin to argue back and forth. She tried to smooth things over by saying, *"Reese he does love you. He asks about you all the time."* I retorted, *"Yea right!"* Finally I broke down and asked her, *"Don't you remember when we were kids and dear old dad came and picked you up? He was not supposed to take you without Dora being there? Don't you remember the horrible name he called me? Or did you just choose to forget?"* I think Nina was afraid to answer. So I said, *"Let me refresh your memory. HE CALLED ME A LITTLE BLACK BASTARD!!! Does that sound like a Father who cares? You really think I believe he even gives me a second thought or gives a damn about what the hell I'm doing in this world?"* Nina was ghostly quiet for a while. Then she softly said, *"Reese I don't claim to know how you feel nor can I begin to understand your pain. I just want you to love him and see him like I do."* I felt sorry for her and I did not know what to say at that moment. Finally I said, *"Well don't call me and ask me to feel anything for this man, my grandfather, aunts, or anyone else on that side of the family."*

It's like somehow that intense conversation went in one ear and out the other. Several weeks later she called me again to share that one of our aunts had passed away. She even dared to ask me if I was coming to the funeral. I could not believe what I was hearing. I immediately told her that I was not and then told her to give my condolences to the family. I also expressed the fact that I would send flowers because most of these people did not care if I was physically there anyway.

Trying to explain to my sister the challenge of surviving even while being alienated and called names like, *"Black Bastard,"* was difficult. I told Nina that instead of throwing that hurtful comment back in my father's face every time I saw him, I chose to turn the other cheek. I decided to move on with my life, but of course I could not forget the reality of what I experienced. To this day I still do not feel like my sister understood. It was like talking to a brick wall actually. She somehow felt like I had lived the better life, even though she had a relationship with my Father. She never understood my feelings towards him and always preferred to make excuses for his mistakes and for his family's ill treatment of me.

TIP 9: *Patience, Patience, and More Patience*: Learn to have patience with your children. They are bound to make mistakes that, is part of growth. You made mistakes when you were a child right? Patience is the process of loving them through those times. It is the only way that they will know that they can begin to trust their actions. They must know that even when they make a mistake the world will not come to an end but that they can live to see another day. The only way that they are going to know this is by having a parent, caretaker, or mentor show them that it's ok to go through a process just as long as they learn from it.

Chapter 10: My Aunt's Hurtful Words

Hurtful words

If you spit in my face

If you pummeled my brains

If you bruised me continuous

It would be your shame

The world would be captured

An audience that could see

The evidence of abuse

That you caused to me

But when you speak words of shame

They tear down not build up

Then the scars are internal

My shame bleeds at the touch

Rudo

How do you begin to illustrate the type of person that my Aunt Lynn was? The solitary thought that enters my mind, is that all my life people frequently whispered to me how much I resemble my father's sister instead of him. That should give you a good indicator right? That also probably explains why when I first met my Aunt

Lynn I was completely awestruck. My first thought when I saw her was *"she is so beautiful."* She was tall and slender with a model physique that resembled mine. Coco-brown skinned, like my sister, complemented by a crown of stunning hair like Mrs. Peters. She looked more like my grandmother than her father, and *"boy was she a feisty one!"* From what I observed, she did not back down from anyone, and this included her brothers.

I have always thought that my sister and Aunt both being strong personalities, would bump heads. If I had to trace the source of this discord I believe that perhaps Aunt Lynn might have been a little jealous of Nina. This can be more clearly understood against the historical backdrop. As a baby Nina came in and took her spot as the baby girl of the family. This would explain in my opinion, why she and Nina had such a love-hate relationship. Aunt Lynn could be paradoxically accommodating of me in the presence of family but uniformly rejecting of me in the presence of friends. I could never understand her vacillation as it related to change of attitude. Although we never were close I did love her despite the things that she said or did concerning me in public. My preference would have been to resemble my Father, and concurrently have my Aunt's attitude towards life, and take no prisoners, determination.

During one of my numerous weekend visits with my sister Nina, my Aunt Lynn took both of us with her to visit a friend. When we arrived at his apartment, I remember the guy making a fuss over my sister (Nina) and telling my Aunt how pretty she was. I stood behind Nina like I often did when we went places and I was unsure of myself or my surroundings. Aunt Lynn's friend then asked, *"Who does the cute little girl belong to?"* Oblivious, I doubted he was talking about me because he never looked my way. My Aunt cheerily chimed, *"Oh this is my brother Ray's little girl."* I can still remember the scene like it was yesterday.

We eventually walked up the stairs and entered this strangers' house. I sat down on a green Ottoman across from my Aunts friend, and my sister and my Aunt sat on a couch across from him. At some point during the casual babble between my Aunt and her friend, he casually leaned close to her. He then whispered attempting concealment, *"Who is the little dark one?"* I will never understand why I was always referred to that way. My Aunt Lynn then whispered the shocker of all shockers *"That is Nina's half-sister her Father's name is Joe-Joe"* At that time overhearing that statement was complex given the fact, he was a man I had never heard of before. This was news to me because all this time I was under the impression that Ray was the father of both Nina and I. At that moment I felt a huge lump start to develop in my throat. I thought at any moment I was going to suffocate. At that exact instance I just wanted to get up and start running down the long flight of stairs that we had just come up. I clasped my hands together and jammed them between my legs just to keep from shaking. I squeezed my legs extra tightly together because if I had not I knew any second I was about to bolt out the door.

I could not believe what I had just heard. All I could think was, *"Oh my God my sister and I don't share the same father. Who is this other man my Aunt is talking about and referring to as my father?"* All these thoughts and more were racing through my miniature head. I not only felt scared but also so extremely alone. What was worse, my Aunt Lynn didn't miss a beat when she made this reference either. Every ounce of my being just wanted to tuck my tail between my legs and go home. Was my sister able to hear this? It was hard to tell since I didn't see a noticeable reaction from her? Was I just hearing things? When we finally left I cannot explain how glad I was. I was now labeled as *the other*. The other what? Was anyone else anxious to leave besides me? I kept searching the faces of my Aunt and sister on the drive back for answers but I saw nothing that provided answers. Nina talked to me like she always had. Maybe she didn't hear the man's name after all. Then again it was just a whisper between friends right? Going home I was frantic and couldn't wait to tell my mother what my Aunt had said to this man about someone else being my father. I knew I had better prepare myself since, Dora always asked me what went on when I was with my sister.

On this day she could clearly see that I was unusually shaken and upset. I often got the feeling that even though she wanted me to get to know my father's family she yet remained skeptical and overprotective. She was probably nervous that they might say something stupid or mistreat me in some way. Call it mother's intuition. As soon as my feet hit the door I just blurted out *"Why did you lie to me? Ray is not my Father."* My mother of course didn't have a clue what I was talking about. She immediately grabbed me and tried to calm me down. I then blurted out the details of the story and what my Aunt Lynn had said to her friend. Tears were streaming down my cheeks during this entire episode. Then when I stopped and studied my Mom's face, her eyes let me know just how furious she was.

After a pause to regain her composure she began, *"I am so tired of those people denying you child. I mean, they were not there when your Father and I were together. Know that you are Ray's just like Nina is. I would never lie to you about something that important. Don't you ever forget that, ok?"* She didn't say anything about the guy, Joe-Joe, who my Aunt Lynn had mentioned. After accepting what Dora had said to me, I was able to breathe much easier. At this point I honestly didn't care if Ray was my biological father or not, I just wanted to keep Nina as a sister. Nina was always going to be my sister because we shared the same mother. Who cared about Ray? He had never taken an interest in me anyway. My life would surely go on.

Years later, I learned that the person that my Aunt had referred to that day was actually my younger brother's father. Regretfully, I admit that seeds of doubt still endeavor to sneak into my mind. From who did I inherited my nose, because it's so much smaller than everyone else's nose in my family? If there was any trait that I undoubtedly inherited from my father, it would probably be his dark skin. Still, I could have inherited that from any dark skinned man. I sometimes wonder where I get my drive and determination from or my sensitivity and passion for talking. I like to think that I got many of my traits from my strong-willed, loving grandmother. The truth is that I really don't know, it's too hard to tell.

Sometimes I feel nothing, just lost and empty. It's like staring at a blank screen and trying to visualize the image that once beamed on the canvas.

So what's the rest of my story? Does it end in tragedy or triumph? I have a loving husband and wonderful children, and for that reason alone I can feel vindication. This victory is often short lived however as I still sense somewhat remorsefully that in some ways my children have been deprived of a piece of their legacy. Legacy in part is the past but also combines the prophecies of their future. The future thankfully tells of blessings that are yet to be lived. But in the meantime while I anticipate this dream-like future, I am left to mourn their fragmented past. And further, I still sustain a certain degree of anger because my father chose not to be a part of my life?

TIP 10: *Discipline and the instilling of Morals and Values*: Teaching your child discipline and instilling moral values is the most important aspect of loving a child that you can provide. Teach your child that character is so important that it will define who they are. Let them know that there are consequences for every action and that it is better to be a leader than a follower. If a child chooses to tarnish their name, and damage their character than they will risk losing everything they have.

Chapter 11: Ronnie

Father

A father is a loving man

Someone who is always going to be there if you need a hand

What a heavenly father

A guardian angel and guide to me

Someone I can count on to be by my side

Seeing him at my games screaming and yelling very loud

I know I'm his son and he's very proud

Knowing in my heart that I make him proud

Hugs and kisses to show how much he cares

Because I know he's always going to be there

Faithful trustworthy yes he is

That's why I'm honored to have him as my father

But most of all my friend

Taray

Not having a father affected every area in my life, particularly when it came to relationships with men. One thing I noticed was, that even with regards to my husband whom I know loves me more than life itself, I was still very guarded. In other words, it remained hard for me to open up and share intimate and personal feelings with him.

Part of my hesitation and reasoning for putting up internal walls was fear of totally trusting a man with my heart. With regards to my husband I found myself thinking, *"Yes I love you, but I will never give you the opportunity to hurt me, you will never abandon me, because I am my own protector."*

First of all I wasn't allowed to date until I was sixteen. As matter of fact early on, I really didn't care about relationships with boys and as a result, probably came off as very aloof. I think that for many of the boys my relative apathy related to dating, provided a challenge. I have often heard young men say in reference to dating that they prefer to be the pursuers as opposed to having women simply fall at their feet. I recall for many years being very uncomfortable around men because they symbolized a dynamic of my past that was difficult and volatile for me. Even as a teenager visiting with friends whose father's were present in the home, I felt fear and apprehension while around them.

When I was finally allowed to date one ground rule was that I had to be in charge at all times. When I met my then future husband Ronnie we started off as casual friends. We quickly became good friends. Well actually, I would say we were Best, Best friends. As I recall I was casually dating someone else at the time, but found myself quickly smitten by Ronnie. One of the things that set him apart was the fact that he was a caring man which is a trait that was particularly attractive to me given my background. He also hung onto every word that I spoke which caused me to feel very valued as a woman. In terms of feeling safe around him I sensed that my best interest also became his best interest. He always seemed to look out for me and what was going on in my life. In all fairness, he was also dating someone else at that time, but I realized even as friends, we interacted well. Having a male in my life that wasn't overly judgmental ensured that I would not feel embarrassed when I shared details about my life at home.

When he did become overprotective at times, even though part of me felt safer, I found myself pushing him away. This response goes back to my need to always be in control of my environment and relationships. As a result I did not want him telling me what to do, or even who to be with. Many of our arguments were rooted in his desire to protect me and which was often overridden by my need for independence. This might appear confusing, given the fact that I had searched many years for a Father that would protect me and look out for my best interest. Again it just highlighted my conflicting feelings and emotions shaped from years of pain and unfulfilled expectation.

Ronnie and I, now look back on those memories as children with fondness and amazement. When I first heard Ronnie say those three words that every woman wants to hear I did not feel how I anticipated that I would. When he said, *"I Love you,"* I actually felt sick to my stomach. I had not heard anyone, especially a male, say those words to me. I remember he asked me if I could ever love him, and immediately I said, *"No!!"*

Yet even with my knee jerk response deep within me a love-struck heart wanted to cry out, *"Yes, yes I can."* I hesitated simply because I was afraid of him later rejecting me or possibly even changing his mind about how he initially felt. I wondered, *"How could a boy know what love is let alone love someone like me?"* Yet he did. He professed that he did love me and wanted to spend the rest of his life with me. Was I dreaming? Ronnie, as it turned out was the rock that I needed in my life to survive. He is a wonderful person and I thank God every day that he was brought into my life. I don't know if I could have made it through my teenage years without him. Truth be told, I doubt I could have survived the aftermath of the emotional and psychological trauma I experienced, without him by my side. He has always been the true definition of a gentleman. And hands down he is my *Night in Shining Armor.*

We have known one another since kindergarten, and were actually classmates from kindergarten through the third grade. From the moment our paths crossed again in high school I felt it was our destiny to be together and we have been inseparable ever since. As a disclaimer I want to point out that it has not been a fairytale without obstacles. We do live in the real world and therefore have had to overcome relationship challenges at times like everyone else. Sometimes I wondered and he probably did too how we have survived for such a long time. I suppose it has to do with the fact that we are both able to look at the cumulative of our accomplishments and conclude we are better off together. Regardless of the trials and tribulations we have had to go through, to get where we are today it has been worth it.

I'll never forget our first high school assembly of our junior year. My two girlfriends and I were the new girls at Canton McKinley High School. Ronnie and I had not seen one another since grade school partly due to the fact I moved a lot in my younger years. I actually started my sophomore year at another high school and then was eventually transferred into McKinley. The way the story goes; Ronnie came into the auditorium looking for his best friend, his partner in crime Troy. My two girlfriends and I were already seated. Looking back I am not quite sure why Ronnie was the last to come into the auditorium.

The assembly had not even started yet when a bothersome and juvenile group of guys positioned behind us proceeded to goad us. I guess boys will boys won't they? For instance they would tap one of us on the shoulder and then act as if they were not the culprit as we spun around in our seats. Being the new girls we anticipated the possibility of being hazed a little but nonetheless became annoyed at the continued unwanted attention. Being the strong and independent young woman that I was, I finally turned and blurted out, *"The next guy that taps me, I am going to slap in the face!"* Of course rather than cower in fear the boys were simply amused at my feistiness. Well low and behold Ronnie walks in and sits down next to his friends. This unfortunate young man was totally unaware of what had just occurred, or how annoyed we girls were.

After a few minutes Ronnie began to tap me on the shoulder, albeit lightly. I ignored the first couple of taps but I could feel my emotions swelling within like a volcano. Finally unable to contain myself I swiveled around ready to do battle. I could feel the hotness of my face and my eyes could only see red. I reacted so quickly when I turned around that Ronnie jumped backwards in his seat. Through gritted teeth and with narrowed eyes I belted out, "WHAT DO YOU WANT?!!!" Even though I was infuriated I tried to yell so as to be heard, but not to get in trouble with any school official that might be in earshot. Ronnie looked like a deer in headlights and could not seem to find his voice in order to formulate a response. Meanwhile his friends were bowled over laughing so hysterically it appeared they might fall off their chairs in any minute. I am sure that he thought I was probably mentally deranged but at that moment I did not even care.

Finally after a few minutes Ronnie regained some sense of confidence and asked, "Are you Lavita Wells?" The way that he stammered when he asked the question let me know that I had successfully gained some intimidation points at least from him for that day. I curtly replied, "Yea. What about it?" He responded by sharing that he remembered my older brother from elementary school. He also later added the fact that he recognized my face as being in the same class as he was in grade school. Then I remember him smiling. When he smiled I felt the entire room spin and my heart began to melt like an iceberg in the Arizona sun. Almost instantly I forgot what I was going to do to the next boy that tapped me on the shoulder.

As if the smile wasn't enough he then uttered a line that I secretly later confessed to my girlfriends, stole my heart for good. He said, "Wow Lavita, you have truly grown up into a beautiful young woman." Now just like his friends almost fell off their seats laughing earlier I almost fell off of my seat from the impact of cupids' arrow. Quickly I caught myself. As my mind raced to comprehend what he had just stated I wondered "is he serious or what?" For him to have uttered those words in front of his friends was not only bold it was extremely romantic and engaging. "He's good" I thought. I faintly smiled and uttered, "Thank you." and then just turned around and sank deep into my seat. I remember a smile being visibly plastered across my face the entire assembly. As matter of fact to this day I can't tell you what actually happened in the assembly following that exchange with Ronnie. I was on cloud nine and although I did not know at that time he would be my husband I knew that he had captured my heart. His smile and face would spend many nights thereafter as my companion in my dreams.

Ronnie and I became good friends and on many occasions he would ask me to be his girl. I would always say no due to the fact I did not want to come across as too easy. I also had lingering doubts as to his sincerity particularly given the fact he was a big time jock who could have any girl that he wanted at the school. Why me? I still struggled with nagging feelings of low self esteem and had unhealthy images of myself. Further I believed that I had nothing of value to offer a man, and that my purpose was simply to survive in life. Besides I did not want to deal with the possibility of dating a jock and having to fend off other jealous girls. This was my position even given the fact that he was the man of my dreams. But eventually his persistence, reassurance, and the fact that he was a gentleman paid dividends.

Ronnie's attentiveness and caring nature come from his upbringing. With regard to the other important woman in his life, his mother who he has always showed the upmost love and respect. This is the same respect and loving kindness that he has shown me always. I'll never forget the first time that he walked me home from school. I could tell that one of the reasons that we both felt so awkward was because we were both thinking about kissing. He wanted to kiss me and I wanted to kiss him, but I had made it clear that I would not be the initiator of the kiss. I recall that when we arrived to the alley by my house we both stopped. He stood there kicking dirt with his toe trying to contemplate his next move. I was looking down at the ground trying to make some small talk about school, and anticipated activities for the next day. Then it happened. He said, "Lavita I would really like to kiss you." Of course this would be the one moment where I did not want him to be so gentleman like and was hoping that he would just take charge. Therefore, I could not believe he was spoiling the moment by asking instead of just taking my arm. "Ughh!!" I guess that is just a man for you. I firmly asked Ronnie, "Why do you feel you have to tell me what you want to do, just do it."

When he finally leaned over and touched my lips I thought I was going to pass out right there in the alley. Part of this was due to the fact that we were both so nervous and scared and as a result it was a very quick kiss. Needless to say it was so satisfying and warm it made every awkward moment that we had previously shared worth the wait. We didn't speak after the kiss we just held hands and then he walked me to my door. When I finally got inside my house however, I literally fell on the floor.

On our first real date two very important things happened. One is that he proposed to me and asked me to be his girl forever. The second thing that happened is that I gave my heart to him and decided that I wanted to spend the rest of my life with him. Even though we were just teenagers, he loved me with a love that was well beyond his youthful age. We decided then to wait until he graduated from college to actually plan a wedding. I remember that first date like it was yesterday. He took me to see the movie Endless Love, which was a real treat at that time for anyone who was into movies especially a teenage girl. Following the movie we went to dinner at our favorite hang-out spot, Burger King. Even though that might not be your fantasy for a dream first date, the company and significance of the evening made it an unforgettable night for me. One other major incident that happened following the dinner was an event that ultimately would change our lives forever.

We had just finished our meal and were casually talking about school, life, and our future together and his going away to college. Of course at this point I did not want to hear about him leaving in the fall because he would be leaving me and I did not know what I was going to do. Then suddenly, out of his letter jacket which I sometimes wore

but did not have on that night, Ronnie pulled out a small box
wrapped in silver paper. I just stared at him because I was unaware of
what to expect next. Honestly I was thinking he was going to pull out
a pair of earrings or some non-committal piece of jewelry. But when it
turned out to be a pre-engagement ring also known as a promise ring,
I was stunned. Ronnie said to me, "I didn't have the money to buy
you an actual engagement ring that will come later. Lavita, will you
do the honor of wearing this ring and becoming my wife after I finish
college and I've finished playing college ball?" I just stared at him
with my eyes wide and my heart open seemingly without the ability
to speak. Although my heart was pounding so hard it sounded like an
African Drum line I was overwhelmed with excitement. If he had said
we can go the Justice of the Peace right now I would have said, "Lead
the way." As matter of fact I did not need to have a traditional
wedding nor a father to walk me down the aisle, I concluded. For
what seemed like an eternity I sat there still unsure of how to respond
to Ronnie. "Was he talking to me?"

Finally, beginning to get anxious Ronnie looked at me and asked,
"Lavita can you hear me?" Ronnie knew that I was afraid of being
hurt, afraid that he might abandon me as my father had done. He
constantly tried to reassure me that his love was unconditional and
that he would never leave me. To his credit this reassurance
continued even after we were married. Although it took a long time
for me to trust and believe him I never doubted his motives. Just
knowing he was there for me helped me to deal with my insecurities.

Other than my Uncle and Great Grandfather, I had never experienced this kind of unconditional love from a man before. Ronnie was just a young man, about to graduate from high school and go on to college, yet he seemed mature beyond his years. "Was he for real?" "Was this moment for real?" I sat and looked at him for a long time before I could finally sum all my emotions up and provide an answer. I finally said, "Ronnie Yes I will. Are you asking me to wait for you?" I knew after we graduated he would be leaving for college, which I was dreading. I still had lingering thoughts that he might forget about me while he was away. He is this big time jock and he was a great basketball player. Would his love for me last that long? Would he get to college and forget about all these special moments that we had both shared?

Ronnie and I decided to get married a year after he graduated from The Ohio State University. He had a great basketball career while a student there and graduated in four years with a Bachelors degree in marketing. He and I were now ready to face the world together. We eventually set the date for July 26th 1986. We began planning our wedding his senior year of college. Truth be told I actually started planning our wedding on that first kiss. Little did he know this of course, and he sealed the deal when he presented me with that promise ring, but of course I did not let him know this.

Since I did not have a father in my life and I came from a background where money was scarce, money for the wedding was a big concern. I was working at the time but of course I knew that I could not pay for the wedding without help. Therefore, I was floored when Ronnie said, "Lavita don't worry I've got this thing covered right down to your wedding dress." I had saved enough money to purchase his wedding band. A quick story about the wedding band, I had actually thrown it in the trash by mistake. Ronnie had taken it off for a pickup basketball game and I did not know he had wrapped it in a piece of tissue paper and placed it in my car. I later purchased him another ring but of course it could not replace the sentimental value of his first wedding band.

I later found out that Ronnie had taken out a loan from the bank to pay for everything related to the wedding costs. It was another indication of his maturity and ability to plan the details. He wanted to make sure that my wedding date would be a day I would never forget. He constantly reminded me of the promise that he made to me when we were teenagers. He said I would not want for anything and regardless of the trials and tribulations that came our way, we would face them together. He was very attentive and yet in all fairness there were some pre-wedding snags.

I always joke with him, even today about his bachelor party. I should probably say the great cleaning job rather, that took place before the actual wedding day. Now as you know typically house cleaning and men do not go together. In other words, usually men are not fond of house cleaning but tend to be more on the primitive side. Nonetheless, my groom to be, decided to clean his apartment a week before our wedding. I had packed up all my bridesmaids' shoes and had them sitting in grocery bags in the living room ready to take them to our hometown, Canton. I figured we could take them the following week for the wedding and that would be one less thing for the girls in the wedding to worry about. After his bachelor party, we were preparing to go home to Canton for the wedding. I was looking for the bags with the bridesmaid shoes but was unable to locate them. Inside the closets, under the tables, in cabinets I searched high and low but was unsuccessful. It turned out that he had accidently thrown the shoes away.

Seeing me search frantically for the shoes, Ronnie finally fesses up. "Lavita I know you are not going to believe this or probably want to hear this but I think I know what happened to your bags of shoes. I might have thrown them away as I was cleaning in preparation for the bachelor party." The look on my face that I shot his way must have reminded him of the first time we met in the auditorium, during high school. He continued, "Lavita I didn't know what was in the bags. I thought the bags were trash. How was I going to know it was the shoes for your bridesmaids'?" Of course my reaction was pure emotion.

I was livid, in tears, and in pure shock. I also wondered how in the world the wedding is going to take place. Finally, I was frantic because now my girls did not have shoes to wear. Now you might be thinking why didn't we just go to the mall and get new shoes? The answer is this was actually a time when retail stores dyed shoes. In terms of our given time frame we simply did not have time to get new shoes, have them dyed, and ready to go in one day. Turns out there was one "ram in the bush," to use a scriptural analogy. We were able to find a store in our home town of Canton that stated they could have the shoes ready in time for the wedding. As long as we provided the sizes and style of the shoes, and they had them in stock we could still move forward with everything. The wedding was scheduled for Saturday and everyone was going up Friday so the timing could not have been better. Ronnie ended up paying for all the girl's shoes and things worked out just fine. He also never offered to clean the house again.

You know they always say the groom is not supposed to see the bride before the ceremony. Well, Ronnie and I did not adhere to these rules. We had our first argument or spat you might say on the wedding day! It was scarcely hours before the marriage even took place and it was of all places in the church. Both of us were very nervous that day and frankly our nerves were frazzled. My youngest sister ShaRhonda, who was my second flower girl, had been sick during rehearsal and was doubtful for the actual wedding. Not knowing if she would be able to be a take a part and walk down the aisle, naturally I was concerned. We were all getting dressed at the church and everyone was running around like crazy trying to make sure that everything would go according to plan. We wanted to stay on schedule and time was winding down for the wedding to start.

To add to the pandemonium my hairdresser had not yet arrived and the time of the wedding was quickly approaching. My hairdresser was traveling from Columbus Ohio. My bridesmaids and I were dressing upstairs and meanwhile Ronnie and the groomsmen were dressing down in the church basement. The videographer had begun filming the pre-wedding events and I personally I was a basket-case. I found myself continually looking out the church doors for my hairdresser. Ronnie kept coming upstairs and yelling through the doors, "Did you give her the right directions?" This of course was a question that was being asked of someone who even today is still bad at giving directions. Now in all fairness everyone knows that my sense of directions also remains an area of weakness. Needless to say I responded by saying, "I gave her the directions you gave to me." Ronnie by now had arrived at the top of the stairs and was trying unsuccessfully to open the door to the room where my bridesmaids and I are dressing.

Finally, I became soooo fed up and frustrated about the possibility that my hair will not get done, that I quickly moved towards the door. I was tired of him yelling through my door, ranting and raving about nothing. As I started to open the door everyone around me was yelling, "No, No, No you all are not supposed to see one another before the wedding!!" Overcome with emotions I started to cry. Prying open the door I stood there in my slip and under garments standing in front of Ronnie. My bridesmaids were attempting to shield my scantly clothed figure, by jumping between us.

Ronnie then calmly said, "If you gave her the directions then they are the right ones and she will be here soon. Just take a deep breath and calm down." With that surprisingly reassuring statement he spun 180 degrees around and left. My bridesmaids and I stood there stunned, but I was not really all that surprised because that is just how my Ronnie is. He is always loving and understanding even when he is racking my nerves. His ultimate objective I know is to ensure my happiness even during those stressful times. Just as the door closed it quickly reopened and in walked my hairdresser. From that moment on the wedding proceeded like clock-work.

I had a huge wedding just as Ronnie and I had planned. There were six-bridesmaids and groomsmen. There was also my maid of honor, which happened to be my sister-in-law, and my husbands' best man, his younger brother. In addition, we had a junior bride, my younger sister, a junior groomsman, along with my nephew as ring bearer. Finally, we had two flower girls that consisted of my baby sister and my husbands' niece. The cherry on the cake was the fact that my Uncle Ernest was the one that gave me away. I look back on that day and see how truly special and blessed it was because all the people I loved were there to participate. I appreciate the fact that I have our wedding video, Ronnie and I make it a tradition to watch it every anniversary. It reminds me of the love that I have not only for him, but for the ones who have now passed on. We have been married for over twenty two years now and we are still as much in love today as we were the day we first met. It is truly a divine appointment when two teenagers who had not seen one another since grade school, years later just happen to reconnect.

In hindsight I am truly grateful for the transfer to Canton McKinley High school my sophomore year. Whatever forces that brought us together truly worked in our favor. We were destined, I believe ultimately to be husband and wife. Shortly after I had gotten married, I had the opportunity to attend a friend's wedding. I watched as her father walked her down the aisle and gave her away. He stood there a picture of fatherly pride and joy. There was a look of love in his eyes. You could see there was also some reluctance in his eyes knowing that he was about to put her future in the hands of another man. It brought back memories of my own wedding. I had seen my father a couple of months before my wedding. My sister Nina had to have mentioned to him that I was soon to be married. He jokingly made the comment about walking me down the aisle. I just responded by saying, "Yea right!"

I could feel myself tensing up because deep down inside I wished it were true. How I wished he had been a father to me and could have walked me down the aisle on my special day. I wished that he could have been proud enough to say, "I've been in her life from the time she was born, and I took care of all her needs. Now I have the wonderful privilege of giving her away to you. Take care of her and love her as I have, because today I'm giving away a piece of my heart-my daughter."

Although this was my wish deep down inside, the truth was we had no such connection. I remember panicking at the time because I had no one to walk me down the aisle. I felt embarrassed and hurt and didn't want to have a formal wedding. I remember even asking my grandfather to give me away but he declined stating that he was too old and would be too nervous. Subsequently I reached out to my Uncle Ernest. I thank God for him because he said he would be honored to walk me down the aisle. I felt so proud having him next to me. He looked at me with such pride and love, expressions I had never seen in the face of my father.

As expected my father never came to the wedding. A small part of me actually hoped that he would show up. It would have symbolized that at least he somewhat cared for me and was happy to support me in that special moment. I wanted to tell him, "Look at your beautiful daughter now, and what she has become. I have found true love and a man that cares about me. This is regardless of the fact that you were not able to, due to unresolved personal issues, be there for me." Perhaps then we could have begun to bury the hatchet and start a new future from that moment forward. But alas it was never to be. He never walked through those doors. Consequently, although it was a day that was filled with joy, his absence caused my heart to sink a little bit.

Life did continue to move forward for me. Several years later I saw my father again, although by now my family had grown. I had conceived children of my own and had begun to celebrate milestones in their lives. The celebrations again would bring with them feelings of emptiness and would reopen old wounds for me. When I should have been happy, I often found sadness was my companion and tears of pain smudged my makeup. There were times my crying was so forceful I almost proceeded to vomit. The pain of not having a father in my life was overwhelming. It would have meant the world to me if he had simply acknowledged me as his daughter. I had pushed those feelings so deeply down inside, it took the love of a husband to revive that desire for fatherly affection. Later on when my children arrived they also stirred within me that long suppressed hunger for affection.

For years I pretended I didn't care, but deep down inside I had been carrying a very heavy and broken heart. I don't remember ever receiving gifts or cards for birthdays from my father or his side of the family. All I got was bags of hand me down clothes that had once belonged to my sister. This practice of hand me down clothes became something I detested not simply because I was better than anyone else but solely based on the symbolism that it held for me. Therefore, I never passed my children's clothes down from one child to another. I wanted each of them to feel special in their own right.

As a child I used to think I was not worthy of new things. I guess my father's family thought they were being generous simply by giving me my sister's used, gently worn clothes. I suppose their logic was that even though the clothes were not appropriately fitted it did not matter. One special piece of clothing that my sister had was actually something that I desired. She had this beautiful white rabbit fur coat. She always looked so pretty in that coat. I used to dream about waking up on Christmas day and finding a beautiful white fur coat just like the one my sister wore. Tragically, neither the coat nor the love found my house, my tree, on Christmas Day.

On a brighter note, my husband always made Christmas and the New Years' Holiday a special occasion for both my children and I. New Years' Eve is particularly a special time because we celebrate it at home as a family unit. Ronnie will cook a lovely dinner and we all sit down as a family. After dinner we watch TV, listen to music, dance, and begin a countdown as midnight approaches. Of course we also had to watch the famous Dick Clark show. As music evolved my kid's became enthralled with hip-hop. Seeking a compromise I would often toggle back and forth between several channels so I could appease their musical taste and mine. In the end it is usually Dick Clark who holds us audience the last few minutes of the countdown into the New Year.

I can remember on one particular occasion my husband and I kissed at the commencement of the New Year as we have always done. On this particular New Year's night however, he grabbed our eldest daughter and began to dance with her. It reminded me of when he used to dance with them when they were very little. They loved to stand on his feet and have him dance them around the room. This New Year's Eve my oldest daughter was twelve and I could really see the bond that she and my husband shared. Through his eyes I could see how much he loved his daughter and wanted nothing but her happiness. I wanted to freeze that picture perfect moment in time. Almost instantaneously I began to cry. I realized that I had missed out on so much as a child. I still hold that picture of my husband and oldest daughter dancing, in my memory. Every time he dances with our daughters, I am so proud of him for being the man that he is and the father that I know they can always depend on. That is what makes Ronnie so special and that is why I had to dedicate a portion of this book to honor him.

TIP 11: *Be a Dad First*: We view you as the best and greatest ever, Dad's of the world. Our hat is tipped to you. Further, we appreciate all of the many roles that you play. As children, we know that often you will also serve as our friend and confidant, but we most need you to be a father first. Someone reading this might wonder what a father is supposed to be. A father in my opinion is not a person of perfection but rather one who is willing to make a commitment. Ronnie was a father who did not shirk his responsibility but made the choice to be in the lives of his children. Although he is kind and fair with them, he also knows how to be consistent and firm. Firm does not denote being domineering either. You can discipline your children without destroying the very fiber of confidence that makes them unique to who they are supposed to be. A father is a man coming to the realization that the character of his children is shaped by his decision to either be active in their lives or not.

I cannot imagine my husband Ronnie not being in the lives of my children. His connection with both his daughters and son will ultimately give them the security and confidence to know that they can make it, because daddy believes in them. If a child sees a two-parent home with a mom and dad both playing their part, that is equally important for them. Unfortunately this is not always the case. Sometimes people separate and that is a tragic and unfortunate reality. Yet even if my husband and I represented a blended family, I still believe that the presence of a fathers love for his family cannot be overstated. I was fortunate enough to have a man whose mere presence provided therapy both for the souls of my children and me.

Even though for years I found difficulty in making peace with my Father, Ronnie has helped me on the journey. He may not have even realized how his involvement with our daughters has caused me to have hope and healing. Many times even in this chapter I have mentioned the tears that I cried and how many walls I put up. But the reason that I ultimately gave Ronnie my heart is because I trusted him. I trusted him with my life and my whole heart then and I continue to trust him now. Although I cried tears of sadness, my tears also represent my process of healing. Walls have come down with each tear that I have cried. Walls have come down with every memory experienced with Ronnie that reinforced the way that a healthy family is supposed to be.

I found myself at times reverting back to those childhood moments and allowing the little girl in me to feel again and let her know her feelings were valid and safe. And ultimately I know that my children have benefited from observing Ronnie. They now understand the true definition of what a GOOD father is supposed to be. Here is my advice to Father's out there. Father's don't dwell on the past but rather look to the future. You may not have been there when your daughter or son was young. If that painful fact is your story then rather than let that become a noose around your neck let it propel you forward. Grow from it. Learn from it. Understand that the decisions of your past are who you were and do not have the power to hold you captive from being who you are supposed to be. That is unless you allow them to be. You can still be a Daddy First, but you must make that conscious decision to allow that desire to propel you forward. Even on my wedding day I was still willing to allow my father the opportunity to show me that he had changed and wanted to be part of my life. He was the one unfortunately who chose not to take advantage of that chance. Although your relationship with your children will change with age and experience, once you prove to be a good father most of the time children will embrace you in that role and love you like you cannot imagine.

Chapter 12: Seeking Forgiveness

Pieces

Pieces of hearts

Splatters of rain

Moments of peace

Mountains of pain

Memories emerge

Disappear again

Forgiveness

Wanting you speaking

Words like, "I wronged you"

I would accept it

Even if I didn't want to

But fearful that spoken

Will be only obligation

Would you ask it from a deep place?

Or only as a mention

Dad either you love me

And accept me till the very end

Or I'll release this burden

And our timeline will just... end

Rudo

There is a biblical passage that really captures the essence of the value of children. It is found in Proverbs 17:6 and it reads, *"Children's children are a crown of old men, and the glory of children is their father's."* It in essence speaks about the fact that children represent the greatest treasure that a man can have. Meaning the child is eternally connected to their parent from a biological standpoint, but also the very nature and tendencies of a child are a reflection of who the parent is. Think about it, how is that children who have never met their Dad, can have his tendencies and behaviors?

That is why many times when a child is introduced they are referred to as so and so's son or daughter. A last name is an inheritance that has unequalled value. If your father was a drunk, someone might say, "You are going to grow up to be a drunk just like your father was." If a father is not active in the lives of his children then he does not gain the privilege of seeing and connecting with what makes his existence truly magnificent, his children. I don't care how successful he is in other areas he is still filled with a void and awareness that his greatest treasure has not been fully realized. It can only be realized as he embraces that God ordained role of fatherhood.

Picking up from where I left off in the last chapter I want to reflect on the experience of seeing my father some years following my wedding. At the time, my son was approximately a year old and I was pregnant with my third daughter. I was in Canton at the time and had gone to pick Nina my sister up for church. She had decided that this particular weekend she would like to attend church with my family. My husband and I arrived at the house to pick her up so we could ride to church together. After pulling up to her house, I proceeded to get out of the car. Shutting the door behind me I then walked up to the house where she was staying. My trek to the front door was suddenly interrupted by the voice of someone calling my name. I could immediately tell who it was by the tone of their voice, and my heart immediately began to quicken.

At first I pretended as though I did not hear him. Determined he called my name again. At that point I decided to respond, "Who is calling me?" Ray my father was congregating in an alley with some other men, and it appeared as though they had been drinking. Ray responded, "You know who is calling you, it's me Ray, your father." My first thought was anger and frustration. How dare he pretend that I should know his voice and further stir the pot by referring to himself as my father? It was hurtful because for years I had longed for him to identify with me as a daughter and father should. Publicly not only had he not acknowledged the fact that I was his daughter, but in addition to his refusal many members of his family treated me as a second class relative.

"What do you want Ray," I shot back? "I want you to come over here" he responded. I tried to move but my feet appeared cemented to the ground. At that point seeing my hesitation Ray began to walk toward me at the same time my sister Nina was walking out of the house. By the time she got out the door, Ray had almost reached me. "Hey girl," he started… "You look good… I know you heard me calling you." I still was unable to move or even utter a word of response. Prior to that moment, every time our paths crossed, it was hard for me to speak. I always had a huge lump that would start to develop in the back of my throat. Nina finally broke in. "Leave her alone, Ray." Then without hesitating, my father just reached out grabbed me and gave me this big bear hug. I stood there utterly confused and shocked. He then blurted out a statement that I thought would never come out of his mouth or that my ears would ever hear. He uttered the words, "Reese, please forgive me."

I thought I must have been hearing things but he repeated it to make sure that I heard him clearly. As matter of fact he repeated his request, that I forgive him twice, while maintaining his grip on me. I was stunned. I was so stunned that I thought I might faint from the sheer force of his hug. I attempted to pry myself loose while simultaneously trying to digest what he had just said.

Finally, after a couple of awkward minutes of my sister looking at both of us, I regained my composure. I spoke words that seemed to come not from me but from someone else. "I forgave you a long time ago, Ray." I spoke it in such a matter of fact way, I think we both could not believe it. At that point I just wanted him to let me go. I wanted him to go away and I felt like running as far away from his as I could. What more could he want from me I wondered? Total redemption of the time lost? Not possible. Never in my wildest dreams had I expected this moment or his initiation at asking forgiveness. In asking for forgiveness he was admitting to me that all of these years he had been wrong.

Finally my father let me go. He then said, "Thank God, Thank God!" I just gazed at him with a puzzled look on my face and wondered, "Why are you thanking God?" "Were you thanking God because you believe that all those years of denying me, and being out of my life all have been forgotten?" Right about that time my husband finally emerged from the car. He began to walk towards us and asked "What's going on." Before my father could say anything, Nina said, "Oh he's just feeling guilty." My husband innocently asked, "Guilty for what?"

I looked at my sister and gave her the look that said 'Nina leave it alone and let it go!' My father was standing there with this blank look on his face. I was thinking to myself, 'Does it bother you that I have someone standing in front of me that loves me and is willing to stand up for me? I have someone who is willing to be the man that you were never willing to be?' Finally, my father said to me, "Reese, one day you and your sisters and I, the four of us, are going to have to talk." That is the first time I have ever heard Ray refer to his other daughter as my sister as well. I didn't say anything because words could not at that moment capture the hollow feeling within me. I should have been happy. He had finally asked for forgiveness, he had finally acknowledged me in his own way. He had finally refereed to Nina and his other daughter as my sister's, and yet I just felt numb inside.

My husband began to pull me by the arm and all of us started to walk towards the car. My father followed. I had never formally introduced my husband and my father to one another. I decided to take this opportunity to do so. I wanted him to acknowledge, what a great man I had married, someone whose love was real and unconditional. I wanted him to see that my husband had provided me with love, safety, and security, things he had never given to me. I wanted my father to see what it meant to be a man and a father. My kids were in the car. Nina said, "Look Ray, Look at your grandson." Nina was truly proud of her nieces and nephew. As she gestured toward my son in his car seat, my father immediately leaned over and kissed my son on the cheek.

I remember feeling such rage at this gesture, but could not immediately trace the source of my anger. Maybe it was due to the fact I had never received that type of affection from him. I wanted to yell, "Get away from my son! He's not your grandson. You are not my father and certainly not my children's grandfather. You don't even know them or me. You have never even been a part of my life. Where were you when I was crying for my father? Where were you?" I felt ashamed and selfish inside. I felt even worse given the fact that he had just asked for forgiveness. Didn't I tell him that I forgave him a long time ago?

I was simultaneously confused and hurt at the same time. My husband gently but firmly pushed my father away from my son. Ray quickly responded, "I did not mean any harm. I would not hurt him." Didn't he know that he had already hurt him by hurting me all those years? He had hurt him by not being in my life and not being a part of me. He had already hurt both of us by not loving and accepting me from the moment I entered this earth.

My father walked away with his hands outstretched toward the heavens. My husband thought he might have been praying. I thought to myself, he should be praying because he has missed out on so much of my life and the lives of my children. The emotions that I felt that day were a combination of anger, confusion and sadness. I resented the fact that he chose to wait thirty years to ask for forgiveness. I wanted to know what was significant about now. Why now? I was angry that he went over to kiss my son, to try and be a grandfather. That did not seem a privilege that he deserved given his rejection of me. Sadly, that was the last day I would see my father. I have often wondered if he had meant what he said about sitting down with Nina and I to talk. What were we going to talk about? What were his motives? Why now? Sadly, I will never know the answer to those mysterious questions.

TIP 12: *Always be in your child's life:* Ray had the opportunity to ask for forgiveness and acknowledge that I was his daughter but chose to wait thirty years. There may be Father's out there who have been waiting for that perfect opportunity. Sadly, it does not exist. I will never know what Ray wanted to talk to Nina and I about. Since none of us know when we will leave this earth, we need to make amends today. Many of the tips may sound somewhat familiar and that is ok. Repetition is the mother of all learning and my desire is to provide simple and helpful tools for men around the world. If you let extended periods of time pass without acknowledging your children with a phone call or a visit then they will have huge memory gaps. Although they may eventually forgive you as I did Ray the internal feelings are difficult to reconcile. Looking back I know that Ray must have felt like a tremendous burden was lifted when I said I had forgiven him. Perhaps he did not feel worthy of forgiveness. It could have been the fact that he decided not to acknowledge me because I was darker than my sister, not embraced by his family and therefore an embarrassment to him. Does your child represent an embarrassing time in your life, Dad? Regardless of the situation that brought them into this world they are still looking to you for value. Think about it. If you were a local sports hero you may disregard that as an incident with little value. But as you remain involved in the life of your children they hear those stories and that represents value to them. Your son or daughter might say, "Hey my dad won a soccer championship while he was in elementary school. Maybe I can play soccer like dad, or some other sport and be successful to." What if you are a father that has spent time in prison or made the wrong choices? Let your child know, admit that. You become an authentic and real person to him or her. Think about it this way, children have very real and grown up emotions just like adults do. There are children today who are being bullied and teased at school. If you are not around Dad then who is going to talk with them about how their day was? If you are not around, Dad, who is going to help them sort through those difficult decisions that life brings? I wonder how many children might have made other choices, had their fathers been in their life. I was one of the fortunate ones who survived despite some very real and difficult struggles.

I could have been a mother on welfare, with six kid's and three baby's daddies. Not that there is anything criminal about that reality, but it makes survival difficult. It makes raising children difficult. Especially given the high rate of Father's who like Ray don't want to claim their children. Finally, understand that when a child looks in the mirror they ask a couple of key questions that only you can help them answer, Dad.

1.   They want to know 'who am I?'

2.   Then they want to know whose am I?

3.   Finally, if you are not involved in their life, they want to know 'why was I not important enough for my Dad to spend time with me?'

Chapter 13: The Day Never Came-Death came Instead

Lost Love

You never said you loved me nor held me in your arms

Claiming you is the man of the house yet causing the family harm

Through the tears and the pain I am still filled with love

Because I have a Heavenly Father who reigns from above

He taught me to forgive and said I'm the apple of his eye

So no, I don't need you; God has taught me how to survive

I pray your heart is changed and your mind renewed

Because an eternity without God is Hell and Damnation for you

G. Caliman

The phone call that I received from Nina came on September 2, 2002. It was to inform me that our father had passed from this life into the next. His death, although unfortunate, finally helped me to close a very painful and confusing chapter in my life. It both saddened me and yet released me from the hurt and pain that I had carried around for so very, very long. When my sister called and delivered the news a wave of emotions swept through my body. I could feel myself shaking as the words came slowly out of her mouth. She had called me so many times with the grave news of other family members before but this was different. It was interesting that prior to that phone call I wondered how I would react to his death, if I was still alive.

I could hardly grip the phone as she continued to share details of his death. Was I hearing right? Ray was dead? I tried so desperately to stay composed because I did not want her to know that I was feeling anything at all inside. The surface was calm, but underneath my waters churned violently, I cried internally. God what is the matter with me. Did I really care that he was dead? He didn't know me and I didn't know him. I spoke in a calm voice so as not to let my sister suspect my true emotional state. Then I began to chide myself. What is the matter with me? My heart cannot be made of stone? I thought, 'Reese girl, you do care, you do feel and are saddened by this news.' Still I could not let Nina know this.

I asked Nina what the cause of death was. She indicated that she was not sure. I wanted to run and scream out loud. "Why, why?! We had not had our talk. You left, Ray and yet you promised." I wanted to get off the phone. I could feel my skin become clammy and I felt like I was beginning to panic. The conversation seemed like it took forever. I think she was waiting for me to respond with some type of emotional outburst. Maybe she had already gone through her own grieving process and secretly hoped that I would be willing to open up and grieve as well. Well she was sadly mistaken because I was not going to permit such unwarranted emotion. As our conversation ended, she promised to call me back with the details and the funeral arrangements. I hung up the phone and immediately called my mother because I anticipated that my sister would call her next.

When I called my mother and told her that Nina had informed me of Ray's death, my mother became hysterical. She immediately began to scream and cry, sobbing uncontrollably into the phone. Did she feel like me? Had old memories resurfaced for her as well? Had she felt the rejection that I had always felt? At that point, hearing my mother open up in that way triggered something in me. The tears suddenly bogan to freely flow for me. I finally acknowledged the hurt and disappointment that for years had been captive within me. That stubborn part of me tired to impede an extended emotional outburst but the pain and tears were too powerful now.

My mother sat and listened to me crying on the phone. I shared with her the fact that I hated my father and his entire family for abandoning me. I shared the fact that my tears were not related to his death but rather Ray's refusal to get to know me as a person, his daughter. I cried because he never tried to get to know his grandchildren until his time was almost up. I was denied his love and affection because his own life, happiness, and well being were more important to him than his daughters.

As I stated before I often wondered how I would feel or react to the death of my father, Ray. Now I know. If I could tell him I would say, "Daddy I cried, I cried for me and you, Daddy I cried for my children. I cried for a lost relationship that is never to be realized." My daughter was listening as I spoke to my mother and I felt her softly tap my shoulder. She brought me a tissue to wipe my eyes with. I could tell from her silence that she did not understand why I was crying. Still, the empathetic look in her eyes told me she loved me and that everything would be ok. She patted me on my back and left me to grieve. Even though she could not comprehend the immensity of that moment, her simple touch reached my heart.

Speaking slowly to my mother through tears I firmly said, "Going to the funeral is out of the question, even if Nina herself were to ask me." Immediately following that moment my thoughts turned to my father. I tried to picture how he looked based on the indistinct image that I had of him. Several years had passed since our last meeting and I could not remember his face. Our last meeting was when he pleaded with me for forgiveness and said one day we would talk. This was his singular plea one that would never manifest into reality. Why? Again I cried. He never would have the opportunity to know his grandchildren now. Not now or ever. I hung up with my mother and continued to mourn. The tears began to flow silently now as they had throughout my life. On numerous occasions I sobbed inwardly. Today would be no different. I would let all the emotions of rage mixed with sadness settle into my heart like sand on an ocean floor.

A couple of weeks went by and with it my father's funeral date. Of course I did not attend. One day a letter came in the mail that was addressed to my husband. When my husband opened the envelope he immediately brought it to me. It was a neatly laminated obituary. I am guessing that it came from someone who probably saw my name in the obituary. As unlikely as it may seem they did actually put my name in the obituary and subsequently felt I might want a copy. These thoughtful individuals who sent the envelope were probably unaware of the circumstances surrounding the relationship that my father and I had. They were uninformed and therefore unable to act in a sensitive way, just like my elementary teachers who insisted I make a Father's Day Card.

As I cautiously removed the obituary from the envelope, I was suddenly startled by the picture. For one I had never had a picture of my father. Also, I had not seen or had contact with him in years. I held the picture in my hand and just starred at it for what seemed like an eternity. I could not stop looking into my father's face. I knew in my heart what I was trying to do. I was looking for any resemblance that might be evident. I was trying to see myself in him, his eyes. Sadly this picture would not solve that mystery, I could not find the connection I so longed for. There was simply...nothing.

Undeterred I continued to stare at the picture. Ray looked like he had lived a hard life. A lot of drinking, perhaps medical problems may have attributed to his appearance. Guilt may have also been the reason that he looked much older than his fifty-six years. I concluded that I disliked the picture. I took the picture and went to the mirror with it. Again I starred at it. I put the picture up to my face and looked at the image of myself and my father's image side by side. I saw nothing. I wanted so badly to find something that confirmed that he was my father. Nothing, no resemblance at all.

My eyes and subsequent cheerless expression reflected in the mirror, was also an image that I could not recognize. Suddenly I had an idea. I called my four children into the bedroom. I proceeded to sit them down and show them the picture. I explained to them that the man in the picture was my father, their grandfather, and that he had recently passed away. Each child asked to hold the picture. Then they looked at the picture and then they looked at me, as I had done earlier try to find the resemblance. Finally my eldest daughter spoke up admitting she could find none. "I wish I could have had the opportunity to know grandpa when he was alive," she admitted. Softly I agreed, "Me too sweetie, me too." I then hugged each one of my children and told them that their grandfather would have loved them too. Looking at the picture once more I put it carefully in a box of keepsakes that I have.

As I close this painfully difficult chapter of my life I realize that it provides the opportunity for me to open up a new chapter of my life. I realize that for all the pain I have also been blessed with salve for the wounds. The salve has come from the comfort, support, and love offered by my wonderful husband, late grandfather, and Uncle. These three special men have shown me the true definition of unchanging love. Now granted I will never understand why my biological father never held me in his arms. I will never understand why he never wanted to nurture me as a child. Perhaps he was a tortured soul that had not found peace with his past. Maybe even though he had his parents and family he did not feel that they truly accepted him as he was and had pent up bitterness. Maybe he simply regretted some of those choices made during moments of youthful exuberance. Whatever his reasoning I resolved my issues and made peace with him long before his death.

I do feel the pain of longing for his love only to be unfulfilled, and accept that this is a reality of my past. However, knowing that my husband patiently loves me even when I sometimes reject his love is a peaceful cool breeze on the dessert of my dry soul. I have no doubt that Ronnie will always love and support his children and his grandchildren. The cycle has been broken. I see that Ronnie has been the key to brining joy overflowing. I am at peace. My children will be the byproduct of a new tradition. Their tradition will be one that is born out of pain, but it will be a new tradition nonetheless. Indeed there is nothing stronger and more powerful in a child's life than **A Father's Love**. Take it from me.

TIP 13: *Remind your children that they are blessed:* Another biblical passage that is a point of reference for me is Psalms 147:13, "He has blessed your children within you." This allows us to know that God has already given favor to children that is specifically for them. This I believe is regardless of what choices parents have made. Despite the choices that Ray made, I would still say that my life has been blessed. Even though he chose not to be involved in my life I was yet given life on this earth. As a result of being allowed to live and be conceived I now have four beautiful children of my own and a husband that loves me. It has taken many years to fully comprehend why I am blessed but it is a beautiful realization. Children will often feel like they come from a shameful background and therefore do not have an inheritance of blessings. It is important that if your mother or father has an embarrassing or non traditional past you are still blessed by God. Your mom may have been a prostitute. This is typically not viewed as a career worthy of honor and respected in society. But given the fact that women find themselves in that situation for many reasons it is important to understand what that means for the child. If you are a child of a parent with a shameful past start off by listening the positive qualities in your life.

1. If you have the use of your limbs you are blessed.

2. If you have some type of roof over your head then you should be thankful.

3. If you have freedom to walk out of that place that you stay and go to the store be grateful. Many young people today are stuck behind bars and every aspect of their lives is monitored.

4. Finally, always remember no matter how difficult your past is it can mold you into a great leader. This is because you can decide like I did that you are going to withstand the vices that oppressed family members. Decide that you want a better life for yourself. I did and ultimately I manifested that vision of a family that I first conceived of when I was young.

5. Remember that many a great leader from politician to pastor, from Doctor to accountant came from humble beginnings. They decided that they would be Master of their own destiny. Don't be afraid to grab a book that talks about the qualities of leadership. Leadership principles can come from many sources and knowledge applied is power. Don't give up you can do it. You can achieve whatever you set your mind towards.

Chapter 14: Father's let Your Children Hear Your Voice

For What

For what is a flower without a seed?

What is root without a tree?

How can a child ever be free?

Without being acknowledged by you and me?

Rudo

*F*ather's are responsible for both blessing and teaching their children critical life lessons. As a Father, your children are bound to follow in your footsteps. Personally, I have seen my family go through so much suffering simply because we lacked the vital love of a father. We were deprived the opportunity to be both blessed and taught by our fathers'. From a generational perspective, my grandmother never received the blessing of her father, nor did her daughter or granddaughters. As a result of the absence of that valuable impartation, most of us have been forced to chart our own paths in life. Our survival then subsequently has been the result of love that came from other people, who have invested in us. So then, as we honor and acknowledge those that were instrumental in our personal growth, it is equally if not even more imperative, to acknowledge how instrumental faith in God continues to be. Through sheer faith and determination alone, we have persevered through countless obstacles and setbacks.

The historical root of our struggle goes back to the time period of slavery. From a careful study of slavery then we are enlightened in terms of recognizing that slavery can take on many forms. The most easily recognizable form at least that, which is frequently observed, pertains to the physical bondage and limitations. This was often the curse and course of our ancestors. Today there are many women and men who yet struggle from a symptom referred to as *"slavery of the mind"* and also *"slavery of their past."* As a weapon of defense, my family, especially the women, have had to maintain a strong will, and a *"can do"* attitude. As such we have determined never to stray from our chosen courses of action, regardless of the frequent obstacles. Despite those advances, today, there are numerous young girls and boys that have not reached the same doctrinaire conclusion. This can again be attributed to past generations dropping the ball and therefore in the absence of impartation the present generation, deals with personal frustration. For many youth they are still waiting by the windows and doors of their houses to hear the sound of their father's voice, and to be embraced by his love.

This often creates an appalling cycle of dysfunction that continues generation after generation. Rather than facilitate the advancement of society, it leaves the vestiges and remains of a generation defined by misguided children. Easily they are identified as ones that will undoubtedly grow up without security, love, or even a sense of identity. So armed with this knowledge I pray that as a Father you fully comprehend the necessity of teaching your sons and daughters. Show them that they are destined for greatness praise them for simply being who they are.

In the same token let me also serve notice to the Mother's. Given the fact that it took two people to "tango", Mother's there is an equally important role that you play. It is not solely the creation of a child, from a biological perspective, that determines the success of a child. Love and emotional support from both parents becomes essential. Now before you quickly spurt out the fact that *"You love those children,"* let me assure you that this is not what I am referring to. The flip side of that coin is that you need to also let the father love those children. By doing so, you show that child not just your love, but also empower them with the impartation from the father which is equally important. In order for this process to become an effective tool, it behooves you to avoid actions which will sabotage Dad's efforts to love those kids. Especially, when you consider how indispensable a father's love for his daughter is in terms of building her character. I've always gotten angry when I see how a mother can sabotage a father-daughter relationship or even serve to derail an equally important and significant father-son relationship.

Now, granted there are fathers that need to do more, and be more involved, but at the same token there are father's that are already going the extra mile. You have many fathers' for example who love their daughters' dearly and are always searching for ways to remain actively involved. Their love is expressed not just financially but also as they provide both **emotional** support and *material* security. *Emotional* support and **material** security are broad terms with multiple interpretations but the essence of such involves providing love and also the necessities of life. Such a father can be defined as one who is teaching his daughter about developing a moral compass which will guide her in the establishment of personal and ethical life values. He is also committed to being her protector and nurturer. Not to mention the fact that he is doing everything a responsible father is suppose to do including paying child support. As a matter of fact, you have some father's who have never missed a payment. These responsible actions should clearly show you that he wants a relationship with his children.

Why does it seem that the child always has to pay the price when the mother-father relationship goes sour? It is a well documented fact that a relationship can end for a variety of reasons. This includes divorce, due to irreconcilable differences. Sometimes, it just simply did not work out between the couple maybe it was just not meant to be. Why then would a mother then want to use her child as a pawn? This serves not to bring peace and healing to the relationship, but rather to only manipulate and hurt the father? Shouldn't the main concern be that the father and child bond not be unnecessarily interrupted or even yet worse broken?

Although a Father's connection to his son and daughter is of equal importance the focus will be on the daughter as she is essential to addressing the primary theme of this book. To have a father who has loved his daughter from the moment of conception or birth loose that connection is tragic. Let's think for a moment, Can you remember the moment when you first told him that he was going to be a daddy? Like innumerable fathers before him his eyes sparkled as he proceeded to become a student of Fatherhood. This studying included, becoming more in tune with the essential requirements of having a new child and supporting the mother. His support and love for her has been unquestionable from day one. You know that you can go to him for anything regarding the care and affairs of his daughter. In return he simply wants to be a part of her life. Although the relationship between the two of you has gone sour he wants to do everything he can for her. In fact by maintaining an active role in the upbringing of his daughter he is also helping you to ultimately fulfill the all important role of parent that you must play. This is due to various factors one being the fact that many children act out more often when one parent is absent.

So again I ask, *"Why would you want to sabotage the relationship built between the two of them?"* This is not about the two of you anymore it's about the upbringing of a child. It is solely about the establishment and maintenance of a relationship with his daughter, one that you both have brought into this world. As a mother you want to make sure that her environment is as loving and secure as possible right? Then why can't you get along with him for the sake of the child? Why can't you simply allow him to operate in his "God-given" role as her father? Why not let him become the father that he so desperately wants to be? Why give him a difficult time over some of the same tired and often contrived and trivial matters?

Does he not pick her up when it's his turn for visits? He's spending time with his daughter. She's *Daddy's little girl.* They have developed a bond a relationship and furthermore in her heart you know he will do anything for his daughter. So why make it so difficult for him?

Are you not getting your monthly child support? If not child support, when you call for financial assistance does he not do the responsible thing and give what he can? You know he makes every effort to see that you get what you need to take care of his daughter's needs. Additionally, does he not go the extra mile? For many Mother's, you not only receive his monthly child support payment, there are additional areas of need that he supports. If for example, you request extra clothing, shoes, or even educational assistance does he not come through? Is she not also on his health and dental plan? Then why do you constantly make it difficult for him by going out of the network plan that has been established by his carrier? Surely you are aware of the added cost associated with that, aren't you? Such a response is typically not done with the child's best interests at all. Rather, it is usually done to because a person wants to be vindictive. Why do you set him up to fail with is daughter when all he simply wants to do is to be able to show his love for her?

You don't? Well, do you include him in her school functions? How about inclusion in, parent teacher conferences, academic decisions, her sports related activities or even in her dance recitals? Do you let him know if there have been any behavioral problems at school so that he can help you lovingly but firmly discipline? Have you thought about putting his name on the emergency forms or do you keep his name off for spite? You know he wants to be there for her but you resist him every step of the way. It's ok that he supports her financially as the law requires and he's happy to do that because he loves his daughter more than life itself. But in your mind it's not ok for him to want to remain involved in her life and why? You are still upset with him that the relationship did not work out between the two of you. So, as punishment you deprive your daughter of the opportunity to know her *Father's Love*.

As she gets older are you encouraging her to write or call her father? Are you building her father up in front of her or are you tearing him down? Acknowledge that there is resentment that you feel toward him. But then you need to move on. Are you hoping that she too will learn to resent him and not want a relationship with him because of your feelings toward him?

I have heard women say there are no good father's in this world, and I disagree. I have seen good fathers going out of their way to be there for their daughters. These good men are constantly running into resistance from the mother because of the failed relationship between them.

Mother's you may think you're solving the problem by sabotaging the relationship between father and daughter, but in the end it's your daughter your hurting by not encouraging and giving her the opportunity to connect with Daddy. She needs to experience the authenticity of a genuine and healthy relationship with a male. She needs to witness a *Father's Love* for his daughter.

There is nothing like a father daughter relationship. Having the love of her father teaches her who she is as a person. Having a *Father's Love* gives her that sense of security that daddy will always be there for me and always have my back. If I need him all I have to do is call. Having a *Father's Love* teaches her how to love and one day receive the love of a man other than her father.

Don't let the cycle continue. Just because you have never known the love of your father please don't deprive your daughter the love of her father. Don't create a cycle of hurt that is often difficult to repair. Don't put your daughter or her father through unnecessary pain. I plead with you from the heart of a woman who experienced the tragedy of not having a Father, "Let your daughter (especially), love her father and let him love her. Build her father up to her not tear him down. Put aside your differences and feelings for the sake of your daughter. With everything she will have to face in her life never let her have to experience not having a relationship with her father and knowing a *Father's Love.* Build him up in front of her instead of choosing to tear him down. Proverbs 17:6 Children are the crown of old men, and the *glory of children are their fathers.*

One final thought that I want to express to both Father's and Mothers is in the form of a story. Before sharing this last very personal story I want to pose a question to you. *"Have you ever felt lost?"* I ask this question because unless you truly look inside yourself and tap into the depth of that emotion then it will be virtually impossible for you to understand how *lost* and helpless children from broken homes can, and do feel. Since they often cannot properly articulate their own feelings I will invite you to peek into my world for a few closing minutes.

At times growing up I felt lost and emotionally bruised. After all, *"How can a child understand the justice and fairness of seeing friends enjoy the bond shared with their parents, when that child lacks those same things?"* Not only will that child get frustrated and envious but as a result they tend to spurn the love of people that *do* want to shower them with love later in life. Is it no wonder that young women, especially, end up in the arms of someone who has a jaded perspective about life and love? There are going to be questions that arise in the impressionable minds of children, in the same way that questions rose up in my mind. They may even blame the other parent, in the same way that I sometimes blamed my biological mother. I thought that perhaps she had done something to cause my father to reject me, while he simultaneously embraced my sister. Then the fact that she chose to continue to find affection in the arms of men who seemed to operate within the same pattern of dysfunction as my own father had was virtually unbearable for me. I thought, *"God is being a father that hard?"* A rejected child lives with feelings of remorse and regret wanting to somehow hide in the shadows of the past. Even years later they still yearn for that love of the absent parent, if for no other reason than to gain a few nuggets of wisdom that may at some point help them to mature. In my mind even now, I wonder what lessons he did not teach me, that I needed to know. There are things about being a young woman, a new mother, a wife that are part of that impartation that I never received from him.

I was therefore left to fend for myself, to discover the keys and formula's to life's mysteries on my own. A child never sets out to be a detective, seeking to discover their own identity, and yet many children are thrown into that role as a necessity of survival because a parent drops the ball. As matter of fact often the remaining parent is often so bruised and hurt themselves that they move forward with tunnel vision, trying to mask their own pain. As such, they may only provide sound bite responses or as mentioned earlier seek to drive the other parent from the life of the children. This is just so they don't have to relive the devastation of their past. Neither, my grandmother nor my mother ever really brought up the subject of my father to me growing up. As matter of fact what's worse is the fact that they never even discussed my sister. So this became another dynamic that is part of the often complex equation of broken relationships, involving children. How could they not have told me about someone as important as a sister? Looking into the future, the bond that we were supposed to share had nothing to do with their failed relationship. And at the same time it had EVERYTHING to do with their failed relationship. Does that make sense? When I finally met my father and sister that transition was equally difficult and jarring. I wondered where they had been all of this time. Also, I wondered why I didn't live with them as well.

 Now granted the love of a surrogate parent is a blessing, but it never replaces the absence of a biological parent. As a little girl, I knew my grandmother loved me but yet also knew she could never be my daddy. As matter of fact even prior to meeting my father I often dreamed about that day, and how it would play out. Innately children are aware that there are connections in there lives with important individuals, such as parents, who may not be present. As a result, they will usually relentlessly pursue the answers, until they are resolved. Imagine if a child has this fantasy in their mind of how that encounter will take place and then it turns out to be cold and abrupt like mine was. I mean in that single moment my dream of our embrace, of me saying, *"Daddy, Daddy, I have always loved you and I know you have always thought about me; I knew one day, someday you would come to me,"* was gone. That dream was slammed like a crushed can under the fist of his insensitivity. He simply paid me no attention and his face showed me no love. As matter of fact as he looked past me I could feel my face muscles tense and I felt intense and immediate disappointment. That day more than any the hunger for his affection, love, and protection, was unreciprocated, I was left alien in a strange world.

In this strange world I wanted to see him as I had before in my dreams. In my dreams he stood surrounded by a mist that hid his face. I saw a small silhouette figure, and thought to myself, that person is me. And it was, but as that silhouette figure reached out to grab daddy's hand they could never quite reach nor clasp it. What's worse is the fact that he never reached out to me. My emotions felt like that mist, empty, void of color, and even in that dream I was alone. It turned out that the dream was to be a foreshadowing of what was to come, a fateful future without the love of a father.

Fast forward to my life as a grown woman and thankfully the story has a wild yet satisfying ending. When I found out that my first born child would be a girl I was so elated. I knew that she would never go through the same feelings I had of being lost because I had a man in my life that loved and cherished me, and would treat her the same way. I was with a wonderful man that would love this child and not live in that space of regret. Yet six months into the pregnancy the dream returned. Again I saw myself reaching out for my father's hand. Although I could never place my tiny hand into his, I kept trying. I would later attribute this experience as symbolic. As I was reaching out for daddy's hand I was actually reaching out for his heart. Alas, I never received that love but it did not diminish my desire to have it. This dream and my painful past came full circle as I saw my husband Ronnie take my new born daughter's hand into his.

The feeling of being lost was finally able to abscond. Like a fog that lifts from the valley to the mountains I knew there would be brighter day's ahead. I knew that the love of a father had finally been realized maybe not for me as a child, but I could experience it now and in the future. How? Well as my children interacted with their father I could share those moments with them and finally place my painful past to rest. Granted a child's painful past is never fully forgotten only brought to the place of resolve that like a once frantic wave, now rolls peacefully upon the sand of life's shores. And for that testimony I say, *"Thank God, Thank God for…my husband…who showed my family…our family…what it means to have, **A Father's Love!**"*